Rise of th

Masters

Book Five of the *Dragon Stone Saga*

Kristian Alva

Defiant Press

The Dragon Stone Saga

Original Dragon Stone Trilogy
Book 1: Dragon Stones
Book 2: The Return of the Dragon Riders
Book 3: Vosper's Revenge

Chronicles of Tallin Trilogy
Book 4: The Balborite Curse
Book 5: Rise of the Blood Masters
Book 6: Kathir's Redemption (February 2015)

The Shadow Grid Trilogy
Book 7: The Shadow Grid Returns (forthcoming)
Book 8: The Fall of Miklagard (forthcoming)
Book 9: Sisren's Betrayal (forthcoming)

Dedicated to my sons,
the sweetest little dragons of all.

Rise of the Blood Masters: Book Five of the Dragon Stone Saga (Chronicles of Tallin)

ISBN: 978-1-937361-12-9

Cover illustration: Stephanie Payne Denne

Find out more about the author at her official website: *www.KristianAlva.com.*

Frigid Waste

Snowmarsh

Brighthollow (unexplored)

Elves

Sut-Burr

The Abundant Sea

Miklagard

Northhurst
Dawns

Everwood Forest

Wheatbridge

White Bay

Loyt River

Freydale

Straits of Tival

Stonehill Bog

Dead Man's Pass

Trautt Plains

Pine Grunge

Mount Heldeofol

Highmill

Pinemount

Syrd

Lake Wren

Highport Mts

Dead Forest

Sleita Border (Disputed)

Aonach Tower (Ruins)

Mount Velik

The Death Sands

Fairfort

Morholt

Blackhaven

Ironport

Hrlinda

Ravenwood

Mistfair

Lysa

Nomadic Tribe

Lockdell Barrens

Parthos

Dyrr

Rignus

Fallwick

Mallowgate

Straits of Tremator

Balbor

Persir

Jutland

Vertlake

Grofhaven

Faerroe

Elder Willow

Gardarshlom

Hwit Rock

Redimoor Island

Buttermead

Darkmouth Forest

The Black Sea

Welley Island

Starryford

The Lofa Sea

Durn

Dragons of Durn

Dragons Paired with Riders

Brinsop, f. carnelian dragon paired with Sela Matu

Duskeye, m. sapphire dragon, paired with Tallin Arai

Nydeired, m. diamond dragon, paired with Elias Dorgumir (offspring of Starclaw)

Orshek, m. onyx dragon, paired with Galti Thallan

Karela, f. onyx dragon, paired with Holf Thallan

Starclaw, f. emerald dragon, paired with Chua Hakmorr

Blacktooth, m. onyx dragon, paired with Fëanor the elf

Poth, m. onyx dragon, paired with Carnesîr the elf

Nagendra, f. carnelian dragon, paired with Amandila the elf

Charlight, f. (deceased), paired with Hanko

Wild Dragons

Shesha, f. carnelian dragon

Atejul, m, emerald dragon (offspring of Duskeye and Nagendra)

Part 1: Dark Family Secrets

The Return to the Elder Willow

Tallin and Mugla kept their conversation light as they returned to the Elder Willow. They talked about the weather and other trivial things. Mugla tried several times to start a dialogue with her nephew, but few words passed between them.

Every time the conversation turned serious, Tallin would find a way to change the subject. He was preoccupied throughout the trip and never regained a peaceful state of mind.

Whenever Tallin stopped to hunt along the way, Mugla was left alone in the forest. At first, she was overcome with feelings of isolation, but eventually, she grew used to the solitude. She'd been living among the dwarves for so long that she was used to having almost no privacy. Compared to the claustrophobic, cramped quarters of the Ilighport caverns, the emptiness of the forest seemed vast indeed.

When the weather was clear, they slept under the stars beside a small campfire. Unfortunately, their journey was punctuated by bursts of freezing rain, and

Mugla often spent the night shivering with cold. When it rained, they slept under a tree, or if they were lucky, in a cave. Still, despite their uncomfortable sleeping arrangements, Mugla never complained.

She wasn't about to make a fuss over it, especially since she had invited herself along on this trip. Tallin hadn't been pleased about that, but he eventually agreed.

She had insisted on coming, partly to make sure that Tallin arrived safely, but also to discover more about Tallin and his connection to Skera-Kina, the Balborite assassin who had attacked them outside the dwarf caverns.

They sat by the fire together in the evenings, talking occasionally about the assassin Skera-Kina—the woman who had tried to kill him. She was ruthless; something out of a nightmare. It usually soured the mood, so eventually Mugla stopped bringing it up altogether. Sometimes they discussed happier subjects, like the dragon's nest. This always put Tallin and Duskeye in good spirits. Mugla's voice broke into his thoughts.

"So how do ye think the eggs are doing?" Mugla asked.

Tallin answered with an instant smile. Tallin loved discussing the impending birth of the hatchlings. It was just the sort of distraction he needed. "I'm sure everything is fine, but I worry every minute. I can't wait to see the nest again." Then, absently, "I wonder if any of the eggs have hatched yet."

"That's unlikely," piped Duskeye. *"It's still too early. Once we reach the Elder Willow, we will monitor the nest together until the hatchlings appear. Shesha is waiting for our return."*

Tallin smiled and crossed his arms behind his head. The dragon's eggs had consumed his imagination since he saw them for the first time. Of course, the nest was more than a pleasant distraction. It was the key to the future of the dragon race. In the years leading up to the last war, the dragons were almost exterminated by the evil emperor Vosper. The dragons fled to the desert to hide. The emperor was eventually defeated, but very few dragons survived the war, and there had been little hope for their survival since.

Only a handful of nesting females remained, and the chance that any of them would successfully spawn a clutch of eggs was low. Yet, somehow, Shesha and Duskeye had mated and produced a healthy nest. Shesha's sudden fertility had shocked everyone. Tallin had been ecstatic about the news.

Finally, hope for the dragon race existed! It wasn't just good news for the dragons and their riders; it was good news for the whole world.

"How much longer before they hatch?" asked Mugla. She didn't know much about dragons, for there were no dragons in the dwarf kingdom. Tallin was a dwarf *halfling*. He was the only dragon rider on the continent with dwarf blood.

"It varies a lot, but it usually takes about eleven months," Tallin replied. "Sometimes later if the weather is cold."

"Why, that's nothing," she replied. "They'll be hatched soon."

He shook his head. "Not soon enough for me. I won't rest easy until they hatch. But as long as the nest is safe, then that's really all that matters." Tallin leaned back, and his face darkened. "Do you think Skera-Kina will come searching for us at the Elder Willow? We can't risk her finding the nest. "

"No, I don't think there's any chance of that," she responded. "It's probably just a coincidence that she showed up at Highport while you were there. And she doesn't know where we're going now anyway." She rubbed the back of his hand.

He forced a smile. "You're probably right." He was clearly distracted now.

"It'll be all right. Don't worry so much." Mugla cleared her throat and looked away. She felt like she was lying to him, but she didn't know what else to say. After that, the conversation died, and for once Mugla

12

didn't try to revive it. She decided not to bring up the subject of Skera-Kina again.

Eventually Mugla nodded off to sleep. The next morning, they continued their journey toward the Elder Willow. The days passed by, and on the twelfth day of their journey they were near their destination. Now that they were closer, Duskeye flapped his wings and flew very fast.

Around midday, Tallin said. "I can see the top of the Elder Willow in the distance. We'll arrive before nightfall."

Mugla smiled. "Good. It'll be nice to see Chua again and to get a good rest for the night. There's somethin' about that place that revitalizes my soul... I love the greenery and the trees. It's such a calm place. Being there helps me think more clearly. "

Tallin smiled. "I agree. It's pleasant here. But one has to be tranquil to appreciate it."

Mugla squinted, looking through the trees. She could see a fire blazing in the meadow below. There was a small man covered with a blanket at the edge of the firelight. "Look, I see a cook fire."

Tallin sniffed the air eagerly. "Did Chua make stew? Or am I so hungry I'm imagining things?"

"No, ye're right. He's definitely cooking something good. Mmmmm! I hope that stew tastes as good as it smells." The aroma of stewed vegetables and spicy herbs filled the air, making their stomachs growl. As they flew closer, they saw Chua carefully stirring an iron pot that was suspended from a hook over a low fire. Mugla smiled. "We could use something hot to eat after all these cold nights."

Duskeye flapped his wings, and they descended toward the sacred grove where Chua made his home. After one final flap, Duskeye landed right near the Elder Willow, underneath the tree's hanging branches. Paper lanterns swung from vines that coiled up the tree's enormous trunk. With Tallin's help, Mugla hopped from Duskeye's saddle.

She stretched her back, as it was stiff from riding. Then, smiling, she hobbled toward Chua, pausing next to a small wooden table with a bunch of large wildflowers on it. She plucked a single flower from the bunch, smelled it, and placed it back down. "Sunflowers are so beautiful, aren't they?"

"Chua!" she called out. "Did you set all this up yourself? What a nice thing to do!" She planted a friendly kiss on the spellcaster's scarred cheek. "Thanks for making such a nice effort for us."

Starclaw, Chua's companion, rested close by. "Hello, Starclaw," Mugla said, patting the green dragon's nose. Starclaw purred and licked her hand.

On the other side of the fire, Chua propped himself up on a mound of pillows. He raised his chin to greet them, saying, "Welcome, welcome. We've been expecting you. I'm glad you're both here. You're right in time for supper. I made the stew, but I can't take credit for the rest. Starclaw hung the lanterns and set up the table of flowers. She's a great helper, you know."

"I can't wait to try that stew." Tallin licked his lips. "It smells heavenly."

Mugla nodded and motioned toward the table. "Why don't ye just sit down, dear? I'll spoon up a bowl and bring it to ye." Steam rose from the pot as the liquid within bubbled vigorously; it was filled to the brim with thick broth and vegetables.

Mugla served each of them some stew, pouring the thick mixture into bowls which were then handed out to everyone. Chua stayed on the ground near Starclaw to eat his meal.

Tallin inhaled deeply, took one spoonful, and smiled. "This is so good." The heat scorched his throat, but that didn't stop him from gulping it down.

Tallin gobbled up his first bowl of stew and quickly rose up for seconds, which he went to ladle himself. "This tastes great, Chua," he said.

Chua chuckled and lifted his bowl into the air in a type of salute. "The recipe is simple—just lots of fresh vegetables from my garden. "

"Ye're quite a talented cook," Mugla said, taking another swallow. "Always so modest."

"I'm glad you enjoy it. Have as much as you like. I know you both must be hungry after such a long journey. I don't get many guests in the fall, so it's nice to cook for someone else besides myself for a change."

"How do you do it...in your condition?" asked Tallin, referring to Chua's disabilities.

Chua smiled. "Oh, it's really not that hard. Starclaw helps me with everything. One learns to take care of oneself, I suppose." Despite the blindfold over his damaged eyes, Chua looked like he was staring into the fire.

After a brief pause, he continued, "Life is filled with difficulties, but also with joyful experiences. This life is one that I am best suited to, I think. I've enjoyed my life, though it's come with many sorrows." He leaned back and patted Starclaw's side. "At the end of the day, I wouldn't trade what I've learned for anything."

Mugla gave him a curious look. "Why so serious all of a sudden? Yer life's not over yet, old friend! Ye've got many good years ahead of ye. And who knows? Maybe ye'll even outlive *me!*"

Smiling softly, Chua said, "Yes... perhaps."

Mugla finished her stew and cleaned her bowl in a bucket of water by the fire. Stretched beside her,

Duskeye was already snoring. "So how've ye been, Chua? What's happened since the last time we were here?"

Chua reached out and picked up a slender pipe from his robe before responding, "Nothing much. It's been quiet. I sent Marron and Pinda to Ironport a few days ago, on a hired barge. They are now under the protection of the Shadow Grid. Other than that, I've had a few visitors come by for readings, but it's been quiet for the most part. Usually, I just tend to my garden or meditate by the stream. Our days have been peaceful lately." He stuffed the pipe with smokeleaf and lit it with a whispered spell. He took a puff and let out a ring of smoke.

Mugla watched as it snaked through the air. "So, what do ye have planned for tomorrow?"

Tallin spoke up. "We're going back to the nest. Duskeye and I have returned in order to guard the dragon eggs. I don't plan to leave this area again until after they've hatched."

"Ah, yes," Chua said, taking another long draw from the pipe, "the nest. How is Shesha's brood doing?"

Tallin shrugged. "Still waiting for them to hatch, but... there's no worries. Not yet, anyway."

"I'm glad you're here to keep the nest safe. I've been hearing some threats and rumors thrown about lately."

"Threats?" asked Tallin. "What kind of threats?"

Chua shrugged. "Threats of war, some slaver prattle, mostly. There's some talk that the orcs are going to attack Mount Velik. The greenskins have been acting aggressively outside their territory for months now. There's talk of new hostilities with them. Their numbers have increased, and they're united under a crafty young leader, King Nar."

Mugla flipped her shawl over her shoulders. "I'd like to teach those monsters a lesson they'll never forget. Filthy greenskins."

Chua nodded. "We can hope. I hear whispers. Stories from the occasional traveler. I've tried to see the future regarding this, but it's still too hazy. Nothing is clear."

Mugla raised her finger. "Now, now... let's not put so much faith in gossip. Sometimes rumors are more harmful than weapons; they're only good for sowing fear."

Chua sat up, tapping his pipe on his palm to dislodge some wet smokeleaf from the bowl. Chua's body looked very frail. "That's true. Hopefully, it's just a rumor, and the orcs will decide to stay in Mount Heldeofol where they belong." He motioned to a stack of blankets nearby. "I have some warm blankets and pillows for you both. You're both welcome to stay as long as you like. The remains of the fire will keep you warm."

Mugla stood and went over to the folded blankets and pillows. She handed a blanket and a pillow to Tallin before taking one of each for herself. Snuggling onto the rugs next to the fire, she watched Chua curl up next to Starclaw.

"That sounds good. I'm tired, and it's getting late," said Tallin, stretching and lying on the ground. He was already half asleep.

Mugla yawned. The night was warm, and her eyelids started to droop, too. "Tallin's right. I've had enough chatter for tonight. Let's try to get some rest."

After a few moments, she turned around and spoke to Chua in a quiet voice. "I was hoping to have a private reading with ye tomorrow," she whispered as she pulled the blanket up to her chin.

"All right," Chua replied gently. "Starclaw carries me into the forest to meditate at dawn. Look for me by the creek, near the black oaks that grow along the water."

She nodded. "Thank ye...I appreciate your help." Soft warmth seeped into her tired muscles, and she fell asleep almost instantly.

Chua didn't say anything. He only nodded and snuffed out his pipe. "So it's begun," he murmured quietly, and then drifted off to sleep.

A Painful Past

Aren't ye going to eat breakfast first?" Mugla asked the following morning. "Ye look so thin." She pinched Tallin's forearm, eyeing him critically. "I'm worried ye're not eating properly."

Tallin laughed her off. "You saw me eat three bowls of stew yesterday! Anyway, I'm never very hungry in the morning."

"Be careful out there," she warned. "Keep yer guard up. And watch the weather. The skies are clear now, but there are dark clouds in the distance. It's bound to rain soon, and ye'd best not be caught in a storm."

"A little rain never hurt anyone," he replied lightheartedly, but his aunt didn't appreciate the humor in his voice.

Mugla frowned. "Don't be so glib with me, young man," she scolded. "I'm not so old and feeble that I can't tan yer backside. This is serious. You'd do well to heed my advice."

Tallin started to roll his eyes but caught himself. "I appreciate your concern, but please don't worry about me. I'm not afraid of a little rain, and I know how to avoid danger. I've been doing it all my life."

She rattled on, not really listening to his reply. "I had a nightmare last night. In it, ye were trapped in a dark place, surrounded by bad people. It's a bad omen. There's trouble brewing. I can feel it in my bones. Ye need to be careful. If ye plan to explore, stay in the north. There are reports of outlanders in the south, and I don't want ye tangled up with those dirty bounty hunters."

Tallin sighed and gave her a half-smile. "I'm not going that far. Just out to check on the nest, that's all. I'll be back in the evening, I promise." He gave his aunt a quick peck on the cheek and mounted Duskeye's saddle. "Enjoy your time with Chua." Minutes later, they were in the sky.

"Be careful!" she cautioned again while waving goodbye.

Tallin waved back without turning around. When Mugla could no longer see her nephew's silhouette on the horizon, she grabbed her cane and went looking for Chua. She walked through the meadow and headed out into the forest, following a worn path through the trees. Mugla walked carefully, using her cane to maneuver down the trail. The trees extended outward in a solid green mass for as far as she could see.

The morning air was still chilly, and she tightened her shawl around her shoulders. A small creek bubbled nearby, teeming with tiny silver fish called *kilscups*. Willow trees grew in huddled clusters along the water, their wispy branches brushing against the ground like an old woman's broom.

Mugla lifted up her skirts and stepped through the tiny stream, starting up the slope on the other side. She paused to take a deep breath, inhaling the forest air.

The Elburgian Mountains, their peaks still tipped with snow from the previous winter, rose up in the distance like towering black teeth.

Despite the beauty of this place, she already missed her home in the mountains. Dwarves made their home in caves, not in the forest. Even though Mugla had traveled far and wide, she still felt a pang of homesickness deep in her gut.

Squeaky high-pitched chatter sounded around her, and she glanced up to see green-skinned tree sprites playing in the branches. The tiny creatures flew down and swarmed around her for a moment, decided that she was an uninteresting creature, and went back to frolicking in the branches. Mugla pulled one overly curious sprite out of her hair and tossed it squealing back into the trees.

Distant cousins of the elves, the sprites lived in the trees, eating insects and leaves. The tree sprites were half-faerie, half-nymph, capricious and prankish, just like the elves, but on a smaller scale. There was a large concentration of them in these woods. The sprites were drawn to wild magic, so it wasn't a surprise that so many of them lived in this sacred grove.

The sprites acted as the natural guardians of the area and had various strange powers. They could open certain portals and they collected magical objects, stealing from mortals whenever they could. Though dangerous in large numbers, the tree sprites knew that Mugla wasn't a threat, so they left her alone.

While she walked, Mugla thought about her previous visits to the Elder Willow. She and Chua were old friends, and had known each other more than thirty years. They first met during the Dragon Wars and became good friends.

Despite his declining health, Chua was the only person Mugla trusted for a foretelling. Chua was a mageborn psychic, and nobody had a stronger gift than him.

In fact, Chua was the most powerful living seer on the continent. All it took was a scrying bowl and a bit of magic, and he could look into the future or deep into the past. She asked Chua to foretell her future, and he happily obliged. In return, she made him a few hot meals.

He usually requested a bowl of smashed yams and flat cakes, which she cooked directly over a wood fire while visiting with him. Mugla used to visit Chua every winter and sometimes once again in the spring, but with her growing list of responsibilities, the times when she could come had grown fewer and fewer.

It was past midday when she finally found him, meditating quietly under an oak tree. A small permanent shrine to the earth goddess was set up nearby. On the shrine, there were several candles, fresh-cut flowers, and a stick of incense. The burning incense filled the air with a sweet aroma.

She tottered over to him.

"Who's there?" Chua's eyeless face tilted up, and Mugla flinched. He wasn't wearing his blindfold, which was sitting on the ground near his leg. During the Dragon Wars, Chua and Starclaw had been captured and then tortured mercilessly. Seeing his scarred face uncovered was a glaring reminder of the terrible suffering he had endured.

Mugla touched his shoulder gently, letting her hand rest there a second before saying, "It's me. I'm here now. Sorry to interrupt yer prayers."

Chua reached for the blindfold and put it over his eyes, tying it off carefully. "Sorry... I forgot to cover my eyes this morning. I don't usually bother unless I have guests. I know my appearance is frightful."

She shook her head. "Nay, nay, it doesn't bother me," she lied.

"Would you like to sit down?" He smiled up at her and offered her a pillow.

"Aye, thank ye," she said, taking the cushion from his outstretched hand. She placed it on the ground and plopped down on top of it.

As the day grew warmer, swarming insects filled the air around them. Starclaw and Chua seemed unbothered by them, but Mugla couldn't keep herself from swatting at the annoying creatures.

"Get away, ye little buggers!" It wasn't just insects, either. The air was filled with the constant chirping of birds, the giggling and rustling of the tree sprites, the rush of the nearby stream. With all the noise, Mugla wondered how he could concentrate enough to meditate here.

Chua scratched at his forearm. "The night was cool. Did the blankets keep you warm enough?"

Mugla smiled. "Aye, mostly. I'm used to the cold—the Highport Caverns are downright freezing in the winter, and there's never enough heating oil to go around." She paused and looked up at the tree sprites buzzing nearby.

"*Those* little green buggers are everywhere, too," she muttered. "Shoo! Shoo!" she said, swatting at a sprite that was prodding inside her ear.

Chua chuckled. "Yes, they are. I've learned to ignore them...for the most part, anyway."

"Mind ye, I'm not complainin'. I love it here. I feel rested. Maybe even a wee bit younger. This place does wonders for my spirit."

"That's wonderful, my dear. You know...I sometimes forget that you're a dwarf. You haven't been a young girl for three hundred years, so I'm pleased that this place helps you feel younger." He smiled and paused, tilting his face up toward the warm sun once more. "Would you like your yearly divination now?"

Mugla cleared her throat. "Aye. I need your help to solve a... sensitive matter regarding my nephew."

Chua's hands dropped to his lap. "Why don't you tell me about it? Maybe I can help in some way."

So Mugla began. "I'm so worried about Tallin! He's in danger. A Balborite assassin has attacked him several times. It's always the same woman. Each time he fights her, Tallin barely escapes with his life. They fought again a fortnight ago. She just showed up at the Highport caverns, without any warning. I have no idea how she found him. If I hadn't been there, he'd be dead. I was able to stop her, but our escape was a very near thing. I'm afraid she'll never stop trying to kill my nephew, so I need to find out everything I can about her."

Chua nodded. "I understand. I'll help if I can. But before we begin, I'm curious as to what you know about her already. Do you have any information regarding her past?"

She looked uncomfortable for a moment, and then said, "Not much, I'm afraid. All I know for sure is that she's a Balborite assassin. And she's female, which is pretty rare."

"I see," he said. His expression changed suddenly, and he asked, "Is her face *completely* tattooed—even her head?"

Mugla made an excited movement with her hands. "Yes! Her head is shaved, and there are many tattoos on her skull. She's even got a few on her tongue. I saw them pretty clearly, because she was *screaming* at me the whole time."

Chua's brows puckered in concentration. "The facial tattoos mean that her training is complete, and that she has taken her final blood oath to the temple. She's a Blood Master; the highest ranking assassin. The tattoos take years to complete, and the head is always done last. The priests don't bother giving full-body warding tattoos to lower spellcasters."

"Well, that makes sense, I guess. I could tell right away she was powerful, though her technique leaves something to be desired. She's very crude, only uses brute magic. There's nothing subtle about her at all."

Chua bowed his head slightly and replied. "Mmm... You know, now that I think of it, I've heard of this woman. She has a terrifying reputation. Even the orcs fear her. Her name is used to frighten children in the borderlands. Common folk say she's possessed by an angry goddess."

"Well, those rumors are sown in truth. She's so powerful that it took two of us to defeat her. Skera-Kina is the strongest mortal sorceress I've ever stumbled across. It took nearly all my power just to escape her, never mind trying to defeat her."

Chua pursed his lips in contemplation. "Does she have any family?"

Chua's question sent Mugla into stunned silence. *Could Chua possibly know the truth already?* She hesitated a moment, cleared her throat, then took a breath.

Her stomach churned. *Should I tell him the truth?* Then she sighed. *It's no use trying to hide it, not from him. I might as well tell him everything.* Her voice came out in a whisper. "During the battle I discovered that Skera-Kina *might* be my bloodkin."

Chua's face didn't register any surprise. In fact, he didn't display any kind of emotion at all. "I see. That explains why you waited for Tallin to leave before seeking me out. Tell me how you discovered this information."

Mugla continued. "When we met in battle, Skera-Kina carried an enchanted blade of my own making. I cast a protective enchantment on that sword years ago, but I'd forgotten about it. Only my own kin can touch the blade with their bare flesh. Skera-Kina and Tallin both touched the blade without injury. I didn't tell anyone else about this. Obviously, the revelation came as a huge shock. Even now, I have trouble believin' it's true."

"Sometimes object enchantments will change over time. It's not a precise form of magic. Are you absolutely certain that Skera-Kina is related to you?"

Mugla wrung her hands. "I thought about that possibility, but I'm *really* good at weapon enchantments. That's no lie. I've never had one go sour before." She sighed. "But maybe ye're right. I guess I'm not really certain of anything. Even now I doubt myself."

"Let's try another avenue. Describe her appearance, besides her tattoos, I mean. Did her features look familiar to you at all, like you could be family?"

Mugla shook her head. "No, I didn't see any resemblance. She's not tall, but she's not short either.

She doesn't look like a dwarf. I assumed she was human. Those rune tattoos cover her entire face, so I couldn't quite imagine what she looked like underneath the markings. To be honest, I was just trying to keep from getting killed. We barely escaped that fight with our lives."

"How about that enchanted sword?" Chua asked. "Where is it now?"

"Tallin's has the *Sword of Sedaria*. I gave it to him as a gift. He knows the blade is enchanted, but... h-he doesn't understand the exact nature of the enchantment. I never told him the whole truth." The last sentence came out reluctantly.

Chua fell silent. After some thought, he said, "I have a solution for you. A *heritage spell* should work. I can use it to discover your kinship with this woman. It's a simple spell for someone who has the Sight, easy for me to perform and quite accurate, too. But in order to perform the spell, I must have an object that Skera-Kina has touched. Anything that has her energy will do. Do you happen to have something we could use, besides the sword, I mean?"

Mugla reached inside her apron and drew out a charred fragment of leather about as large as her thumb. "After Skera-Kina left, I stepped outside the mountain and found this." She handed it to Chua. "It was on the ground near the area where we fought. I know it's hers. I hoped it would be of use to ye."

He rubbed the leather between his fingers and sniffed it. "I sense magical residue." He sniffed again and wrinkled his nose. "And burnt flesh. This was soaked in blood. I can smell it."

"Ye're right," said Mugla, glancing at him. "It was still bloody when I picked it up. Her skin is fused to the leather."

Chua's eyebrows arched up. "Remarkable. What spell did you use to restrain her?"

"I trapped her using an ancient spell: *paralysis fire.* The counter spell is simple, but there aren't a dozen spellcasters alive who know it. The spell just isn't used much anymore. To be honest, I gambled on her not knowing about it, and luckily for me, the gamble paid off."

"I've never heard of paralysis fire being used in battle. Isn't it used mainly as a restraining spell for prisoners and such?"

Mugla nodded. "Aye, it only restrains an enemy. Once someone is trapped inside the fire circle, they're safe from harm. The spell isn't really designed to be defensive, but that's also why it succeeded with her. I chose it on purpose. Paralysis fire allows a weaker mage to trap a stronger one—it can incapacitate even the strongest mageborns. She tried many counter spells, but none of them worked. The Balborites wouldn't bother teaching their apprentices a passive spell like that."

"Did she attempt to escape the fire circle?" Chua asked, mostly to himself. "That would certainly explain the blood."

"Right again. She tested the boundary of my circle several times, and each time, it burned her badly. The pain must have been terrible, but she kept trying anyway. I smelled her burnt flesh in the air as we ran away from her. She never stopped fighting the spell. And every time she tried to break the circle, I felt weaker. She tried to break the circle with brute magical force. She's as nasty as they come, and very skilled. Breaking a fire circle from the inside takes immense power. She eventually escaped, because I simply couldn't maintain the spell anymore. She was defiant the entire time, never showed a drop of fear. A league of sorcerers couldn't hold that woman for long."

"Interesting." Chua paused. He rubbed the leather in his fingers and said, "This item will suffice. But be warned. This isn't an everyday object, like a shoe or a piece of jewelry. It's got blood and battle residue on it, so it carries a fair amount of negative energy. That shall affect the incantation in a negative way. Many factors come into play when performing this type of spell, and the object itself is quite important. You may see..." he paused, searching for the appropriate words, "*unpleasant things*. You must also understand that a heritage spell only provides a vision of the past, of that

33

which has already occurred. You won't be able to change anything the spell shows you. If the spell is successful, be prepared to face the consequences. It will reveal information about your loved ones, and what you learn may not be positive. There are many paths to the truth, but they are seldom easy."

Mugla reached up and flipped a strand of gray hair from her eyes. "I understand. I still want to learn. I still want to know, whether it's good or bad."

Chua was again silent for a while. "As you wish. Just give me a few moments to gather my strength."

Mugla moved closer, lowered her voice, and said, "Thank you."

Chua tilted his head back and sighed. His fingers fluttered up to touch his gleaming dragon stone. Starclaw sensed the draw of the spell and crawled closer to her rider's side, touching his shoulders with her snout. The stone at the base of the dragon's throat also began to glow. Once their powers merged together, Chua started chanting softly. *"Lita-Hlita, Lita-Hlita..."*

He lifted a corner of his blanket, exposing a bare patch of earth. Uttering words in the old language, he traced a circle in the dirt. He spit in the center of the circle.

A lick of flame shot up, and the air sparkled. A wisp of foul-smelling smoke rose from the circle, and Chua added a handful of small twigs and dried grass, causing more smoke to rise. He was finally ready. When he spoke again, his voice sounded far away, as though he were speaking through a long tunnel.

"The spell has begun," Chua rasped. "I am blind, but I can still see the images in my mind's eye. The vision you see before you comes through my dragon stone. Together, we shall gaze upon the past. Hopefully you will find the truth you are searching for."

Gradually, three figures materialized in the curling smoke between them. There was no sound or smell, just a scene from a long time ago. Mugla's eyes widened. She recognized the dwarf caverns at Mount Velik. The vision showed her old midwife's quarters.

Inside a dimly-lit cave, several people attended a birth. A dwarf female lay on some furs, her clothing covered in blood, her head lolling from exhaustion.

There was a human male in a corner of the room. In the center of it all was Mugla, holding a screaming pink newborn. Mugla looked a bit younger, with fewer wrinkles and a straighter spine.

"Do you recognize the people in this vision?" Chua whispered.

"Aye... all of them. The dwarf woman is my sister, Tildara. She was Tallin's mother."

"And the human in the corner? Who is he?"

"My brother-in-law, Audun. That's Tallin's father. His parents were different races. Tallin's father was human."

Chua nodded. "Yes, Tallin is a *halfling*, isn't he? As for his parents, they're both dead now, right?"

Mugla gulped. "Yes. Audun and Tildara both died during the war." She set her eyes on the smoky vision again, watching as her younger self lifted up the crying baby and quickly tied off the umbilical cord. Then she carried the infant to a wicker basket near the door.

The father looked at the baby and began sobbing, covering his face with his hands. He looked over at Tildara and shook his head miserably. Then the mother started crying, too.

"The baby was a little girl," said Chua quietly.

"Yes," Mugla admitted, her voice hoarse. "I attended the birth, and I delivered the baby. That baby was Tallin's sister...my niece." She choked the last words out, as if it hurt her to admit it.

A panic rose in her chest. Mugla knew what was about to happen. A shudder ran through her body as the terrible memory swept through her. Oh, how hard she'd tried to forget that fateful day! How many times had she tried to erase it from her memory! She didn't want to relive this horrible moment again.

Mugla squeezed her eyes shut for a moment. But she had to watch it. She had to know the truth, even if it was as terrible as she was starting to suspect. Slowly, reluctantly, she opened her eyes and waited for the images to continue.

The smoke shifted and the scene continued. Now the baby's father stood above Tildara, his arms shaking. Pacing, throwing his hands up and down, Audun yelled at her. Tildara was curled into a ball on the floor, rocking back and forth. Mugla stood quietly in the corner and wiped the infant with a moist towel.

Doing her best to ignore the screaming, Mugla wrapped the baby up in a little blanket and offered the girl to her mother.

Shaking her head and crying, Tildara refused to touch the baby. There was a deep pain in her eyes. The father continued shouting, unmindful to his wife's anguish. In the vision, Mugla frowned and left the birthing chamber, taking the infant with her.

Now Mugla was walking through the mountain, her expression unreadable. She kept walking until she reached the gates leading to the outside. There she paused, ordering the guards to open the gates. The guards looked at her with a quizzical expression, but they complied with her request. After all, she was the oldest dwarf spellcaster. Not many dared to question her.

By now the baby had quieted down. Mugla stepped outside and waited for the gates to be closed behind her. She wiped tears from her face and tried to smile at the infant as it reached up for her, its tiny fist opening and closing. She kissed the baby on the forehead. Then she put two fingers in her mouth and whistled sharply. At first, there was no response, so she whistled again. After several minutes, a brightly colored wagon became visible in the distance.

The wagon stopped once it reached Mugla. A young woman in vividly colored skirts stepped out. The woman gave Mugla a wide grin and a swift embrace. Mugla smiled back and handed the newborn to her. The gypsy woman tickled the newborn under her chin, and the baby giggled. There were several children in the back of the wagon, all of various ages and skin tones. Some stepped forward, inspecting the newcomer with innocent curiosity.

Chua coughed, and the vision faded for a moment. His breaths were labored. "I'm sorry. I must rest for a moment. This is a longer foretelling than I'm used to." After his breath steadied and his chest stopped heaving, he said, "I saw that you took the baby to another family. What happened?"

Mugla's shoulders sagged, as though every part of her was being pulled down by some great weight. "Tildara became pregnant during the war... but the father of the baby *wasn't* Tildara's husband. My niece was the product of rape. It was obvious as soon as I lay eyes on that little girl. Tildara was so upset at the time. I understood her situation, so I gave the baby to another family to raise. I thought I was doing the right thing." Mugla started crying. "I've made plenty of mistakes in my life, but maybe that one was the hardest of all.

"This is painful for you," Chua sympathized, placing his hand on her shoulder. There was no hidden reproach in his words. "Do you wish to stop?"

She bit her lip and twisted her hands. "No. I can't stop now. We've come this far already. I've got to know what happened to that baby."

Chua nodded and raised his hands again. The vision returned, but the location had changed. The scene shifted and blurred. Now it was later in the year. The ground shimmered with a thin blanket of snow. It was nighttime, and the same gypsy wagon had stopped to make camp. The family prepared their campfires, huddling together for warmth, heating their hands next to the crackling flames. They were talking and laughing together, and everyone seemed happy. Then the whole group turned around suddenly, with frightened expressions on their faces.

Now, men on horseback were galloping through the camp, knocking over crates and supplies, rounding up the hapless travelers and corralling them into one spot. Dozens of armed men with blue tattoos circling their necks and wrists screamed for the gypsies to surrender.

These were outlanders, ruthless bounty hunters that were paid to gather slaves and hunt down runaways.

The gypsies fought back with picks and shovels, but they were vastly outnumbered. It didn't take long for the outlanders to subdue the entire group. The caravan was pillaged, and all the gypsies were taken prisoner.

The scene changed again. Now there was more snow on the ground, and the sky was winter-clear. The unfortunate captives were standing on the coastline, trembling against the freezing wind. The male prisoners were bound and gagged. Women and children huddled nearby, shivering against the cliffs.

Many wept openly, tears trickling down their cheeks. There, in the center of the group, was Mugla's niece, now several months old. A weeping young girl clutched the baby with one arm and stroked her head with her other hand. The notorious northern slaver, Druknor Theoric, walked up and down the line, examining the captives like animals ready for slaughter.

With jet-black hair and muscled forearms, Druknor was ruggedly handsome. He stopped in front of a teen boy with a bruised face. The boy dared to spit at him. Druknor wiped the spittle away and laughed. He raised a meaty fist and swung it at the boy's head. The teen crumpled to the ground, unconscious.

Druknor barked an order while waving to his guardsmen. The guards jumped off their horses and gathered the captives into a huddled mass before pushing them onto a waiting slave ship. The prisoners were shoved into the ship's hold and sealed inside. Then the ship sailed away, disappearing into the horizon.

Chua gasped and fell back. The vision wavered, and the smoke dissipated. It was over. "That's all there is... the spell has run its course." His voice cracked. Eventually, his breathing slowed, and he sat up again. He looked incredibly tired.

"Did you discover everything you needed to know? I know it is difficult for you to accept, but it is the truth nonetheless."

Mugla couldn't speak. It was all too terrible to believe. *How could this have happened?* Shaking her head, she fought to hold back the river of tears welling up behind her eyes.

Chua placed his hand on her shoulder. "Why don't you tell me about it? Talking will help you feel better."

Mugla rubbed her eyes and sighed. The sun streamed down on her from above, casting dappled shadows on her back. Despite the warm temperatures, she felt chilled inside. An emotional coldness. Finally she spoke. "The truth is worse than I *ever* could have imagined."

"That is often the case with these things," he said sympathetically. "Nobody wants to believe what hurts them."

Mugla hung her head in shame. "That poor baby—my niece—was the result of an assault that happened during the war. Mount Velik came under attack, and the elves offered to help us fight."

The old seer gravely shook his head. "Ah, I see where this is going. It's a common story, isn't it? When elves involve themselves with mortals, there's usually a problem."

"Yes... that's how it happened. An elf fathered the baby. My sister was deceived by an elvish glamour. As I said, the elves came to Mount Velik to help us fight. They did fight valiantly during the war—and saved many lives. We would have lost the mountain if not for their presence. But as ye know, the help of the elves always comes at a price, and a steep one at that. Whenever there was a lull in the fighting, the elves grew bored. And a bored elf is a dangerous elf. They love to manipulate mortal folk, and Tildara suffered greatly for it."

Chua nodded. "It's a common problem. Elves engage in all manner of trickery, and not just when a mortal catches their fancy. I've had my own problems with them in the past. The tree sprites that guard the Elder Willow report back to the elf queen, Xiiltharra. At first, I was furious about it. I have very little privacy here. In time, I learned to accept the situation. There's really nothing to be done about it or any other situation that involves their kind. Elves aren't bound by mortal laws; they do whatever they please."

Mugla cast her eyes on the ground. "It's a lesson that my family learned too late. Back then, I warned my sister to be cautious, but I never expected something like that could happen. Tildara was a married woman! But even that didn't deter them. The elves harassed her constantly. My sister was beautiful and small, with fiery red curls and pretty blue eyes. Her beauty was a curse!" Mugla paused, overcome with emotion. She pressed a handkerchief to her face and wiped away tears.

She continued, "Tildara wasn't like me—she was very shy, so her appearance brought her nothing but misery. Tildara's rejection of the elves only enticed them more. It was a challenge for them—one they were determined to overcome. Our king, Hergung, knew about the problem. Several women had complained about similar harassment, but he let it slide. Hergung needed the elves to fight. We desperately needed their archers and healers. So the problem was ignored. A few months later, one of the elves used a glamour to trick his way into my sister's bed. The enchantment was very convincing. She never suspected that it wasn't her husband lying next to her. It wasn't until the next morning when she went into the pantry that she discovered the elf's deception. There on the floor, drugged and unconscious, was her real husband. Tildara screamed for help. The elf was in her bed, still cloaked in his disguise. He never dropped his faerie glamour, not even as he ran away. No one knew the elf's true identity."

"What happened after the rape was discovered? Did your sister report it to the king?"

"Of course she did! Our entire clan protested. But of course none of the elves stepped forward to confess. Why would they? They acted like it was some big joke! They refused to name the elf responsible for the assault. After this final incident, Hergung expelled all the elves from the mountain, but the damage had already been done. My sister was pregnant. Hergung lodged a formal complaint with the elf queen, but nothing came of it, not even an apology."

"So your sister decided to keep the child?"

"Yes and no. She was traumatized—unsure of what to do. I offered her a potion to terminate the pregnancy, but she decided to have the baby. There was a chance that the child was her husband's, and she didn't want to risk losing the baby if it was his." Mugla sighed and shut her eyes. "Unfortunately... ye could see from the vision... the baby wasn't his."

"Did you know for sure? Were you absolutely certain?" His voice showed curiosity and concern.

Mugla drew a shuddering breath, knuckling fresh tears from her eyes. "Yes, I knew. It was obvious. The baby was a *dwarfling*. There was an otherworldly beauty in her face. It's a rare coupling—a dwarf with an elf—but I've seen enough babies in my lifetime to know the difference."

"It's an infrequent combination," Chua said. "I've only met one in my life. *Dwarfling faeries* have a unique appearance, but it's difficult to place their ancestry unless you know what you're looking for. They look almost human." Chua touched the ground with his hand. "Dwarflings are usually quite handsome. Elves are tall and thin, while dwarves are short and stocky—those physical traits cancel each other out and make for a beautiful child."

"I know," Mugla replied, a wistful smile tugging at her lips. "My great-grandmother was a dwarfling herself, and she was a real beauty in her youth. Her elvish blood is the reason why I've got mageborn powers, and it's probably the reason I'm still pottering about at my age."

"Let's get back to the story," Chua said, patting her hand. "Once your sister discovered the baby was half elf, she decided to give the child up for adoption, correct?"

Mugla nodded. "Aye. Tildara refused to touch the baby. She wouldn't even look at it. It happened so long ago, but it still pains me to think about it. My sister remained in denial durin' the whole pregnancy. She never dealt with the tragedy of what happened to her. She just kept believing that the child was her husband's, and he wanted to believe it too. Neither of them was good at facing reality or at making the effort to heal. My people knew a family of gypsy traders—the matriarch was a sterile woman who adopted lots of children. She was a good mother, one I could trust. When the travelers camped by the mountain on the day of the birth, I told myself that it was fate. I gave the baby to them. I guess what happened afterwards wasn't really their fault."

"What happened to your sister after you gave away the baby?"

"She hated herself," Mugla replied, bitterness dripping from her words. "Tildara became so depressed. She cried for months, partly because of the child, partly because her husband was enraged over what had happened. He couldn't blame her. Of course it wasn't her fault, but he was furious about what the elf had done to her and even angrier at the king's lukewarm response. Audun wanted to declare war on the elves—wanted to fight every one of them. Hergung knew that was impossible, so everyone just tried to go on with their lives. But Audun just wouldn't let it go. He was too angry. He talked about vengeance constantly.

Audun and Tildara started fighting, and their relationship began to unravel. The stress became too much for Tildara to bear." Mugla hesitated. "Then... one day, after another quarrel with her husband, my sister took her own life."

Chua shook his head. "I'm so sorry to hear that. And Tallin's father? Your sister's husband? What happened to him?"

"He went stark, raving *mad.* He was utterly consumed by rage. He already despised the elves—he blamed them for what had happened. But now it became even worse. He wanted to kill them all. The war was winding down, but there were still skirmishes here and there. He threw himself into the fighting and placed himself in constant danger. He wanted to die. Oddly enough, it wasn't even a dangerous mission that killed him. One day, a few months after my sister's suicide, he traveled to the city of Ironport and started a brawl with an elf in the streets. He stabbed the elf in broad daylight and was killed. The elf claimed self-defense, so the matter was dropped. Since Audun fought during the war, he had earned the right to be buried at Mount Velik. Our clan buried him right next to my sister, and that was the end of that. Everybody in the family just wanted to forget it had ever happened."

"Did you ever find out who the father was?"

There was a pause. Mugla's voice grew husky. "No, we never found out. Tildara was dead, and so was her husband, so the whole incident was just swept under the rug. Nobody wanted to press the issue with the elf queen."

Chua settled back a moment. "Does Tallin know the truth?"

Mugla shook her head and cried a little. "No," she finally admitted. "Tallin was only a boy. He doesn't remember. I told him that his parents died during the war, but that's all. I spared him the worst of it. Only a few people know the whole story. After everything that happened, I could barely deal with my own grief. Losing my sister was so difficult for me…" A single tear trickled down her wrinkled cheek.

Chua was silent and seemed to be lost in thought. When he spoke again, his voice was soft and carried no judgment. "So Skera-Kina is of mixed blood, and she is your niece."

"Aye, but I believed she was human, I swear it! The possibility that Skera-Kina was my kin simply never occurred to me, especially not while we were fighting for our lives. But now that I know the truth, I realize that she does look a bit like my sister. There's a similarity in the eyes and the jawline. But I never would've guessed the connection before."

Chua said, "Skera-Kina attacked Mount Velik several years ago. Did anyone ever mention anything, for instance, that she looked like she was related to your family? Sometimes a stranger will see a resemblance where a family member will not."

"Nay, never a word, not even in passing," Mugla replied. "If anyone did see a resemblance, they never mentioned it to me. The elves even tussled with her a few times, but they never said anything to me either."

Chua frowned. "Yes... the elves certainly would have known. They can always spot one of their own, even those with mixed blood. It's probably the reason they didn't kill her when they had the chance. Elves are reluctant to kill anyone that shares their blood, even halflings, no matter what the reason."

"Well, they shouldn't have kept it a secret. They should have said something to us," Mugla cried. "If they knew who she was, they should have told us the truth!"

"You're right, the elves should have told you something," he said softly, "but that information was potentially dangerous to the elves. You're a competent spellcaster, and you're curious about things. If you discovered that Skera-Kina was your niece, with a few extra steps you could have discovered the real father of the baby... and your sister's attacker. There are plenty of spells that are useful for revealing parentage. You know this to be true."

Mugla could only nod. She was too overcome with emotion to trust her voice. In the distance, a wolf howled. Mugla shivered. It was a dark omen, one she wished she hadn't heard. She looked into the sky. It was growing darker, and the afternoon shadows were growing longer.

Chua was thoughtful for a moment, looking up at the darkening sky. "Elves aren't wicked, not really... though it does often seem like they are. They have no natural hatred of any race. They're just impulsive. They don't consider the consequences of their actions. In a way, they're like children, or even animals... except they lack the innocence. They're driven completely by their desires—they're slaves to them. I don't envy them. You know, Skera-Kina is probably unaware of her own ancestry. The Balborite priests may not have shared that information with her. She may not even understand why she's drawn to Tallin. They're brother and sister. It's natural for them to be drawn to one another. They're both powerful mageborns, which means their bond is even stronger than normal siblings. Their encounters aren't accidental. They'll keep happening because of their blood ties."

"Ye're right... I know, I know." She sighed.

Chua gave her an understanding smile. "Don't be so hard on yourself over this. You did the best you could, and your sister's choices were outside of your control."

Gazing up at the sky, she sighed heavily. Dark clouds rolled in from a distance. "The wind's kicking up. It's getting rougher. There's a storm brewing."

"You're right. I can smell it in the air. The storm will arrive before dawn tomorrow morning." Chua reached for her, squeezing her hand. "Look... you tried to spare Tallin some heartbreak. Perhaps you wanted to salvage some of your family's honor, but avoiding this problem has only prolonged your pain. Misfortune falls on everyone. It's best to deal with it when it happens. I understand the burden that you carry in your heart, but you must tell Tallin the truth. You must tell him that Skera-Kina is his sister."

Captured

Duskeye dipped and dove through the clear blue sky, his sapphire-blue wings muscular and rigid as they picked up the wind. Tallin smiled as he clutched the saddle. He felt great.

They flew toward a small cliff at the forest's edge. As they got closer, a solitary cave, its narrow opening scorched and riddled with claw marks, appeared in the distance. Duskeye flew toward it. When they landed, Tallin leapt from the saddle with excitement.

"Great to be back." Tallin said, his eyes glued to the entrance. They waited outside a short distance away from the cave's mouth for the female dragon to wake up from her nap.

Soon they heard scrabbling inside the cave. Tallin walked away, moving behind a large boulder and crouching down behind it. The dragons desired some privacy, and while he desperately wanted to see the eggs, he didn't want to upset Shesha.

Shesha shuffled outside and yawned before approaching Duskeye. She purred and nuzzled Duskeye's neck, and the two dragons spoke softly to one another.

Tallin caught snippets of their conversation, but most of what they discussed couldn't be heard over the light winds. Tallin peeked through some branches and watched Shesha sniff the air before glaring in his direction.

Shesha let out a throaty growl. *"I can smell the fleshling. Your human is here."*

"Yes, he is here," Duskeye admitted, a bit sheepishly. *"We came together."*

"Humph!" Shesha snorted. *"Why do you spend so much time with that fleshling creature? What is he to you?"*

"He is my rider and my companion," Duskeye explained. *"Do you see my dragon stone? See how it is carved? Tallin wears the other half of the stone on his chest. We are bound together for life. Tallin will not harm you, or your nest. I swear to you, upon my life. We are here together for the same purpose, and right now, that is protecting your eggs."*

Shesha's eyes narrowed. It was obvious she would need more convincing. Shesha opened her mouth to protest further, but stopped herself. *"I'm going hunting,"* was all she said.

Duskeye looked relived. He didn't want to have another argument about humans. *"Fly east; you'll find game there. I saw a flock of geese near the beaver dam. They looked fat and delicious."*

"Would you ...like to accompany me?" she asked, fluttering her eyes.

"I would love to join you," he replied, *"but I prefer to stay here and watch the nest. Our most important work is guarding the eggs."*

The female shuffled her feet and nodded. *"I understand,"* she said quietly. *"I appreciate your help, and even the help your fleshling attempts to give, even if he is bothersome at times."*

They spoke in hushed tones for a few moments more, and then Shesha opened her wings and flew away to catch her breakfast. Tallin stood up, brushed himself off, and went to join Duskeye at the cave's entrance. "How is she?"

Duskeye shrugged. *"About the same, I suppose. She's nervous, but not anymore than usual. The hatchlings aren't ready to come out yet. It's colder here than in the desert, so the eggs will take longer to hatch."*

"We'll make sure all the hatchlings survive," Tallin said. "I swear it." Nothing was more important to him.

Ever since he laid eyes on the nest, he couldn't bear to leave it unguarded. Tallin wanted to stand right over the eggs and protect them himself. Tallin peeped inside to catch a glimpse of the eggs.

He was fascinated by the nest, and he longed to touch their smooth shells, but he didn't dare. Of course, the female would never allow it, which is why he kept his distance. Tallin was only allowed at the cave when Duskeye was present.

Shesha was deathly afraid of humans and barely tolerated Tallin's presence. It was already a delicate state of affairs, and Tallin didn't know how much more interference Shesha would tolerate, so he did his best to stay out of sight.

His worry only made the anticipation worse; it was terrible and exciting at the same time. He couldn't wait for the eggs to hatch, and every day he had to spend waiting loomed ahead of him like some vast ocean he had to cross. Despite his fears, Tallin was hopeful. This clutch of eggs was the first he had seen in decades; the first step in bringing dragons back from the brink of extinction.

It was a miracle, but the situation was still very precarious. There was still only a small chance that the dragon race could be saved.

In order for that to happen, all these eggs would have to hatch and then mature into adult dragons.

Tallin was determined to make it happen. *"I'll save them, even if it costs me my life!"*

It was the first time in generations that anyone felt hope about the dragons. Days ago, Tallin risked sending a bird messenger to Parthos, the desert city where the other dragon riders made their home. Tallin notified the riders of the nest's existence. They sent back enthusiastic and congratulatory messages for Duskeye, with a bit of harmless teasing thrown in for good measure.

Everyone wanted to come and see the nest, but Tallin advised against it, advising them that the female was very skittish, which they all understood. He left the nest's precise location a secret. Considering the situation, and what had happened to dragons in the past, he knew that being overly cautious wasn't a bad thing.

Tallin crept over to the entrance again and peeked inside. The nest was huge; a loosely constructed collection of grass, twigs, and soft fibers, all packed together in a disk-shaped mass. The interior was lined with clay, which had dried into a hard lining. The nest was tucked into a corner at the very back of the cave. Ten eggs rested inside, a gleaming rainbow of shining colors. Their smooth surfaces reflected light beautifully, even in the near darkness.

He counted them again. One, two, three, four ... ten. Ten eggs. "It still amazes me to see them. I wish they would hatch sooner though. The long wait is nerve wracking."

"A few may hatch early," Duskeye replied. "They usually do. And when the first ones come out, you'll get a chance to interact with the hatchlings. Dragons have ravenous appetites when they're born, so Shesha will go looking for food immediately. Newborns can't fly until their wing bones develop, so you'll have a captive audience whenever she goes hunting; at least for a few weeks."

Smiling, Tallin walked back to the shade, thinking about dragons.

They stayed to guard the nest until Shesha returned, sitting in the forest shade and enjoying the breeze. Duskeye nodded off and Tallin read an old book Chua had lent him.

All was peaceful, and for a few hours, Tallin was able to keep his mind occupied with something other than his obsession with the nest.

Shesha returned in the late afternoon, carrying a gleaming fish in her jaws. Tallin didn't have a chance to hide before she landed, but she didn't say anything. As usual, Shesha ignored Tallin completely. She merely sniffed the air with distaste, and then shuffled over to talk to Duskeye.

Duskeye rose up when he saw her, but he kept his head bowed with respect. *"Your hunt was a success, I see. Were you able to find the geese?"*

Shesha dropped the fish from her mouth. *"Yes, they were by the river, as you said. I caught a few, but the meat was tough. I prefer younger birds. I went to the lake and caught some fish instead. They're spawning now, so they're easy pickings. I plucked this one from the water like it was nothing."* She smiled at Duskeye proudly. *"This one is bursting with roe, and I saved it for last. It's sure to be delicious. Would you like to share it with me?"*

Duskeye looked back at Tallin, who was now waiting at the opposite end of the cave again, with his body politely turned away from the dragons. Duskeye could tell he was restless. He was tapping his foot so vigorously that his boot was making little clouds of dirt. *"I'm sorry, Shesha. I would love to join you, but I must go. My rider hasn't eaten all day, and I know he's hungry. It would be unfair of me."*

"Humph! That's fine, then. I'll just enjoy my fish alone!" She turned her back and swept past him without a backward glance.

Duskeye sighed and went to join Tallin. *"Well, she's back and as usual, a little bit cross. Shall we go? Shesha will be fine on her own for a while. I could use something to eat myself."*

The sun sparkled orange as it dipped below the horizon. "A quick hunt sounds like a good idea. I'm starving." Tallin glanced up at the sky. There was an odd grey color to the clouds. "There's rain coming though."

Duskeye motioned to his rider, pointing at his back. *"Hop on—we can beat the storm. Small game is plentiful in this forest. We're bound to catch something."*

"All right," Tallin agreed with a smile. "Let's get moving." He grabbed his sword from his saddlebags and briefly drew it out of its scabbard. Flashes of light glinted off the blade. The sword was beautiful, a dwarvish creation and a great source of pride for him and his family. Tallin slipped the sword back into its scabbard and tucked it into his bags.

"There's an open meadow a little farther west," offered Duskeye. *"I've had good luck hunting just about everything out there, including deer and rabbit."*

"Sure, let's try it. Lead the way." Tallin adjusted his saddle and mounted Duskeye's back. They took off into the sky, rising high above the forest canopy.

They flew toward the field, wind whipping through Tallin's red curls. He enjoyed the feel of the air lashing against his skin, the feeling of flying. Again, Tallin grinned and found himself wishing that their flight would go on forever. To touch the skies; to fly into the clouds with the birds—the feeling was absolutely liberating. Tallin raised his face to the setting sun.

At last, he felt happy.

As they approached the field, Duskeye circled down through a break in the trees. Fed by a spring of clear water, a tiny creek flowed in the center of the meadow. Tallin dismounted, knelt down, and scooped bubbling water into his cupped hands. Duskeye joined him, and they drank together.

Tallin spotted a tangled mass of lingberry bushes at the edge of the clearing. Ripe and filled with juice, the berries dangled down from the branches in thick clusters. If the hunt didn't go well, they could at least pick berries. Even from a distance, he could see there were enough of them to fill a dozen baskets.

Duskeye looked around and sniffed the air, a puzzled expression developing on his face. *"Odd. There's a strange fragrance here that I can't identify."*

Tallin pointed to a thicket of vivid wildflowers across the meadow. "It's probably those purple blooms. They have a strange smell. Like cow dung." He crinkled his nose. "They don't smell very good."

"No, it's not that. I can't place the smell, but I know it. I remember it, but from where?" Duskeye looked around sharply.

Tallin shrugged. "Come on, let's get moving. I bet there's plenty of game down that path."

Duskeye opened his jaws to respond, but Tallin was already walking into the trees. Duskeye followed, his good eye moving warily from side to side. The light was waning quickly, and their eyes adjusted to the darkness.

They followed a narrow trail which led deeper into the forest. Tallin moved onto the path, and Duskeye crawled along behind him. Pointing at the path, Tallin said, "I recognize this track. It's an ancient one. If you follow it long enough, it eventually leads to the southern ocean. I've hunted here before, many years ago, before I was a dragon rider. There are excellent hunting grounds here."

It turned dark, and the moon rose in the sky, giving off a silver light. The surrounding forest pushed in on them from all sides, the branches brushing against their bodies. The underbrush grew across the path, forming tangles that made it difficult to walk.

Their progress slowed to a crawl, and Tallin pulled out his sword to slash away obstructing foliage. Overhead, a thick lattice of branches filtered the moonlight to a trickle, making it impossible to tell the time. More and more trees crowded the way, their roots rising up like giant earthworms on the trail.

Tallin squeezed through a pair of saplings with their trunks wrapped around each other.

"There's not enough room for me to pass here," Duskeye said, *"Perhaps we should go back."*

Tallin glanced back. "It's too tight for you, but I can still squeeze through. I'll continue for a while. Why don't you fly back to the field and see if there are any animals walking through for a drink at that creek? Hopefully one of us will catch something."

Duskeye hesitated for a moment, staring at his rider with narrowed eyes. *"All right, I'll go. But be careful out here. There's an energy in this forest that's making me uncomfortable."*

"Don't worry about me. I'll be okay," he replied. "I'll contact you if I catch something."

Duskeye nodded and flew upwards, breaking through the branches above. Moonlight poured onto the forest floor. As Duskeye flew away, he heard the not-so-distant sounds of thunder.

Tallin grasped his sword and moved on. A gray mist lifted up from the earth and darkened the forest even further. Tallin squinted, trying to see deeper into the trees, but it was impossible. He felt more like prey than hunter here, and if it wasn't for the glow of his sword, he might have given up altogether.

Tallin heard another clap of thunder. Carrack! The sound reverberated through the trees. The storm was definitely getting closer. There was another crash of thunder followed by a bolt of lightning.

His stomach rumbled so loudly that it almost drowned out the noise. *I should have gone back with Duskeye and eaten those berries.* But what he really wanted was some meat, something that would stop the growling in his stomach. So he pushed forward.

The canopy closed overhead, forming a dark tunnel of vegetation. The foliage became so thick that the trees seemed to be joined. Tallin's stomach growled louder, but he was ready to give up. The path disappeared. Making it through the forest was impossible now that the path had vanished, and he knew that he would probably get lost if he continued.

With his sword in hand, Tallin sighed and turned around. He'd have to settle for lingberries after all. He took one step and stopped, looking down at his hand. His sword was vibrating at an incredible rate, moving in his palm.

Tallin's eyes widened. A familiar buzzing started in his ears, like a hive of honeybees. His heart pounded and his breath quickened.

"Magic!" he gasped. *There's magic nearby, and it's powerful.* Tallin sent a telepathic message back to Duskeye. "Get out of the forest and go back to Shesha's nest. Wait for me there. Stay alert and remain on guard."

"But why? What's going on?"

"You were right about this forest! There's something wrong here. There's magic, and it isn't good."

"Are you in danger?" Duskeye's voice was filled with alarm.

"No, I'm not. Not yet, anyway. I feel a presence, but I'm not sure what it is. Wait! Something's coming!"

A falcon's cry pierced the sky. Tallin knew immediately what it was—a scouting bird, sent to survey the area. He ducked behind a patch of ivy, doing his best to stay out of sight while he waited for the bird to pass. Tallin stopped moving and tried not to make any noise. He ignored the temptation to scratch a spot where a leaf was tickling his cheek. Peeking through a gap in the foliage, he got a glimpse of the bird as it flew overhead. A streak of lightning filled the sky with a flash of brilliant light, and he spotted a thin gold circlet around the falcon's neck.

This wasn't just any scouting bird. It was an elf spy. He watched the bird circle twice and then disappear from sight.

Even without the circlet around its neck, Tallin knew the bird was an elf spy. Elves could manipulate any animal to do their bidding, but they were notoriously picky about the appearance of the animals they chose. Elves avoided using pigeons or crows, even though they were smarter and more efficient messengers. Instead, they preferred using golden-tailed falcons. Elves couldn't resist beauty, and the falcon, even though it wouldn't be *his* first choice, was breathtakingly beautiful.

Tallin sent a final message to Duskeye, telling him about the falcon, and warning him again to return to the nesting cave. Then he moved into the tall grass, sheathing his sword as he did so.

He took each step carefully, like a thief breaking into a guarded fortress. He didn't cut any more branches. He didn't want to create too much noise or draw attention to his location. If something blocked his path, he went around it. With every step forward, the ringing vibration in his ears grew louder.

His progress slowed to a crawl. The forest seemed to grow quieter, until he couldn't even detect the buzz of insects. It was eerie. The stillness felt unnatural, as if the forest was holding its breath. The noise from his boots tramping over dead leaves sounded deafening in the silence. The buzzing in his ears remained, and it kept getting louder and more insistent.

Tallin didn't think it could grow any darker in this part of the forest, but he was wrong. He stepped into an inky blackness so profound that he could not even see his hands in front of him. After several minutes of fumbling around in the darkness, he came to a small clearing in the trees, where a splinter of moonlight was visible.

Which way now? he thought.

Just then, a family of doves shot through the trees. Tallin jumped with surprise, his eyes darting in every direction. He took a deep breath and moved back into the shadows.

He could hear joyful birdsong in the distance. It was faint, but it was there. He smiled. *Now, at least, I know where to go.* He followed the sound of the birds, knowing they would lead him closer to the source of the magic.

Black clouds rolled over the moon, and soon, rain began to fall, soaking through his clothes. Lightning, bright and jagged, flashed nearby. Despite the freezing torrent chilling his skin, Tallin was thankful for the storm, as the pounding of the rain and the crashing thunder masked his footfalls.

Another hour passed before he saw a glowing arc through the trees. Holding his breath, Tallin crept forward, making his way toward the light. He peered through the trees, desperate to see something that would explain the unbearable din in his ears. He blinked, and a chill swept through his veins.

Elves.

They were in a tiny clearing, surrounded by a bubble of light—Carnesîr, Amandila, and Fëanor.

The elf dragon riders. They were back on the mainland, but why? They were alone.

What are they doing here? And why aren't their dragons with them? None of this makes any sense.

The elves stood in a semi-circle, talking quietly. The ground was bone-dry below their feet, and no rain fell anywhere near them. Carnesîr held a large black bag in one hand. They were arguing about something, their voices sometimes became heated. Cautiously, Tallin crept closer, trying not to make a sound. He stopped inching forward when he could hear what they were saying, but just barely.

Carnesîr set the bag on the ground and opened it. One by one, he drew out ten oval stones. They were polished alabaster, smooth and milky white. Tallin watched as Fëanor stepped forward and swept his hand over them. The stones glimmered for a second, then transformed into a range of bright colors.

The ten stones looked exactly like dragon's eggs.

Air rushed out of Tallin's lungs. He froze, breathing hard, wondering what to do. *Be silent!* His brain screamed at him. *Control your breathing! They must not discover you here!*

Carnesîr pointed at the stones. "Lovely, just lovely. These decoy eggs shall serve us well. Our spies confirmed the number, and our baser cousins have revealed the location of the birthing cave. Those dull-witted tree sprites are good for something after all."

The other elves began to laugh, but Carnesîr held up his hand. "Queen Xiiltharra has made her desires clear. She wants them all. If the glamour is preserved, the female dragon will be completely fooled. Switching the eggs will be easy."

"It might not be as easy as you think. Switching the eggs is a risky gamble," Amandila warned, with a voice so high that it sounded like a rabbit. "If all the eggs fail to hatch, the dragon riders from Parthos will get involved. They'll discover the decoys. You know their spellcasters are competent enough to remove faerie glamour. And then they'll suspect us. We should leave a few real eggs in the nest. If one or two of them hatch, the female will be less likely to suspect anything. After all, in the wild sometimes the eggs don't hatch."

Carnesîr scratched his chin thoughtfully. "You've made a good point. I would prefer to avoid trouble with the mortals." Carnesîr turned to Fëanor, who was leaning against a tree. "Fëanor, what do you think? Should we leave a few eggs behind?"

Fëanor gazed up at the sky and shrugged. "I don't know. None of our options are very good."

"Oh, come on, Fëanor, don't be so difficult. I'm asking for your opinion."

"You know my feelings on this matter," Fëanor replied, irritation creeping into his voice. "What does Xiiltharra hope to accomplish with this little undertaking? If we steal the eggs, we'll anger the dragon riders of Parthos. Even our own dragons are angry. Blacktooth isn't speaking to me now; he's so upset about this whole thing. This mission is a bad idea. I don't like any of it."

Carnesîr flushed, a scowl spreading over his features. "You're speaking quite candidly about our queen. You should consider holding your tongue."

Fëanor gave another shrug. "Well, you asked my opinion, didn't you? I'm just being honest. Let's suppose Xiiltharra makes a mistake about taking these eggs."

Carnesîr shook his head slightly. "Our queen always reacts cautiously with regards to mortal affairs. It's always been this way. Now she feels the time has come to intervene."

Fëanor shot him a disgusted look. "And what are we going to do with the eggs once we get them? You know that dragons can't mate in Brighthollow. Elf magic suppresses their fertility. The eggs probably won't hatch there either. Are we going to just hold onto them forever?"

Amandila nodded her head in agreement. "Fëanor is right. Dragons can't mate in our land, but we could have saved some eggs before, when the nests were more plentiful, returning the eggs to the desert after the human wars were over. Now, it's too late. Only a handful of dragons remain. We could have saved more if we had acted sooner. Why did she wait so long to do anything?"

Carnesîr opened his mouth to respond, but Fëanor cut him off.

"See! I'm not the only one who feels this way!" he cried. "Xiiltharra takes her position of neutrality too far. The dragons are almost gone, and this is the first nesting female we've seen in ages. Xiiltharra's strict policy of non-interference with mortal affairs didn't cause this catastrophe, but it made the situation a whole lot worse. Xiiltharra waited too long to act. You know it, and I know it. This action will only serve to make everyone angry. It's a mistake."

Carnesîr frowned deeply. He took a deep breath to calm himself. When he spoke again, his voice was calm, but the serenity didn't quite reach his eyes. "Ah, I understand your concern, I really do. But there's no changing the past, is there? What's done is done, and complaining won't help. We need to think about the future."

Fëanor snorted. "Fine. What do you want me to say? Take the eggs, then. Take them all. Simple as that. But either way, it's still horrible."

Carnesîr paused and glared at him. "I need solutions that work, not a lecture. Understand?"

"I'm not lecturing you," said Fëanor. "I'm telling you, this mission will have disastrous consequences if it gets traced back to us. If the other dragon riders discover our involvement in this affair, they'll declare war on us. You know how serious they are about saving the dragons. Parthos has declared war for less than this. You *know* how humans get when they're angry. Mortals aren't good for much, but they're remarkably good at getting angry, starting wars, and killing each other over nothing. I'm not quite sure why Xiiltharra wants to go to war with Parthos over some stolen dragon eggs."

Carnesîr puffed out his cheeks. "Xiiltharra doesn't want to go to war, Fëanor! This isn't about the humans. Why are you being so obtuse?"

Amandila interrupted their argument. "How about a compromise?" This time, she spoke so softly that Tallin had to strain to hear her. "What if we only take half the eggs? We could take five to Brighthollow, and five could stay here. That's more reasonable."

Crouching directly behind the elves, Tallin listened anxiously in the bushes. He needed to get a message back to Duskeye, to tell him what was about to happen, but it was impossible for him to concentrate, especially with the constant buzzing in his ears. As he continued to listen, the fear kept creeping up his spine.

Carnesîr shook his head. "A partial solution isn't going to work. Xiiltharra won't be happy, and neither will the dragons. A compromise that only makes things worse doesn't isn't a great idea."

"Maybe our dragons were right," Amandila whispered, her head down. "This just feel so wrong. My dragon said that stealing the eggs is a great cruelty. She believes we should leave the hatchlings with their mother. I tried explaining our motives, but she didn't want to talk about it. She refused to come with me. She's never refused to come with me on a mission before."

"Blacktooth said the same to me," said Fëanor. "Deep inside, we all know this is wrong, no matter how we try to justify it."

Carnesîr gazed up at the branches. The rain had paused, and a glimmer of stars started breaking through the trees. "Look... it's not *wrong*. It's just an unpleasant task. We're doing this for the greater good. The dragons will understand in time. We're doing it to save them." Then his face brightened. "Just think about it. If this plan works, we'll get the credit for saving them! Won't that be wonderful?"

Fëanor rolled his eyes. "Yes, of course!" he said, his voice dripping with sarcasm. "And what a *hero* you'll be in the eyes of our queen. Your motives are always so pure."

Carnesîr's eyes sparked with anger. "What are you implying, *exactly?*"

Fëanor raised his chin defiantly. "I'm *implying* nothing. No. I'm saying it outright, to your face! Since you're Xiiltharra's favorite, then you deal with the consequences. Neither of us wants to be here, so stop trying to pawn this horrible decision off on us."

Carnesîr shook his fist. "I'm not some court *dandy* trying to impress our queen!"

Fëanor spat back. "That's a blatant lie. You're always cozying up to the queen. Let's be frank about that. Now she's come up with this bright idea to steal dragon's eggs and take them back to Brighthollow. And for what? For safekeeping? It's sheer idiocy! What does Xiiltharra hope to accomplish?"

"Enough!" Amandila said, stomping her foot on the ground. Her voice rose back to a rabbit-like pitch. "Both of you, stop fighting! We need to cooperate with each other, not fight like children. Let's decide right now what we're going to do."

"Fine," Fëanor said, "I don't agree with any of this mess, but you're right—the sooner we get this over with, the better."

"Right," Carnesîr said. "I'll decide then. I say we strike the nest tomorrow, at dawn. We know the location of the cave, and the decoy eggs are ready. There's no reason to delay. We have to move fast, and we can't be noticed."

"And the eggs?" Amandila asked. "How many are we going to take?"

"All of them," Carnesîr said firmly. "I'm going to follow our queen's orders. That's what Xiiltharra wants us to do. As you say—I'll deal with the consequences later."

Tallin, who had watched the exchange with rising horror, finally turned to leave. *I've heard enough. I've got to get out of here. I must warn Shesha and Duskeye!*

When he turned into the bushes, his foot slipped. A sharp crack echoed through the air as he snapped a branch. The elves swung around, turning in his direction.

Tallin cringed and froze. He stood with his back to them, heart pounding in his ears, all the time willing his legs to remain still. He turned his neck slowly and looked back. The elves were staring in his direction, their mouths twitching.

"Did you hear that sound?" Amandila asked in a whispery voice.

"Yes, a branch breaking," Carnesîr said. "Someone is out there—listening."

Fëanor walked toward Tallin's hiding place. Crouching low, Tallin waited, taking deep, silent breaths, to control his heartbeat. Fëanor came closer and closer. The elf reached out, spreading the leaves with his hands.

Leaping from his cover, Tallin lifted his hands and shouted the words to a numbing spell. His hands glowed brightly. *"Detta!"* A burst of glittering yellow light shot out and wrapped around Fëanor's body.

"I'm hit!" Fëanor screamed, clutching his legs. "Blast it! I'm hit!" His body crumpled to the ground. The glowing thread swirled and tightened around him like a whip. He let out another howl.

"It's that infernal halfling! Catch him!" Carnesîr shouted. "He'll ruin everything!"

Tallin dashed from the underbrush and sprinted into the forest. Carnesîr and Amandila immediately gave chase, their nimble bodies leaping over the bushes with ease. Fëanor's screams echoed behind them.

Tallin smiled to himself. His spell's effect was only temporary, but it felt good to wipe the smug expression off Fëanor's face.

Tallin ran onward, smacking branches out of his way, moving as quickly as he could. Behind him, the elves yelled a constant stream of threats and curses. Tallin struggled to stay ahead of them.

"Don't let him escape!" Carnesîr shrieked, infuriated.

The elves moved to intercept him. Tallin ran faster. He glanced over his shoulder and saw Amandila snarl, and a gleaming orb of flame blossomed in her palm. She hopped over a log and paused just long enough to lob her firebolt in his direction. It tore through leaves and branches, burning a smoldering trail as it went.

Tallin lurched sideways, throwing himself to the ground, and watched the ball sail over him and into a nearby tree. The tree burst into flames. Tallin jumped up and barely avoided another fireball; it missed him by a hair's breadth.

He took off running again, hoping he could find a place to hide long enough to send a message to Duskeye. If he couldn't, he wasn't sure what the elves would do with him. They weren't pleased. But would they really kill him just to keep their mission secret? Tallin gulped and kept running. They could certainly hurt him... he didn't want to find out what they were capable of.

A huge wall of thorny bushes blocked his way, making it impossible for him to pass. He surveyed the area, but there was no easy way around. He would have to double back, and he didn't have time for that. The elves were moving quick, catching up to his location. He could hear their shouts behind him. It wouldn't be long before they found him. He could feel his heart pounding in his chest.

They would be there any second. Tallin pounded his fist against the wood and heard an echo. The tree was hollow. It was small, but he could just squeeze his body inside. He thanked the gods and wiggled through the opening at the bottom of the trunk. Peeking out through a hole, Tallin watched as the elves ran past him.

That was lucky. A deep breath escaped his lips. Tallin was a strong runner, but he knew that the elves would catch him eventually. Fast as he was, the elves were faster—and more nimble.

His heart still pounding, Tallin touched the dragon stone on his chest and reached out with his mind, trying to contact Duskeye. He felt the dragon's sleepy consciousness responding.

"Duskeye! Duskeye! Wake up!"

"Tallin? Where are you?" Duskeye's voice was sluggish. *"It's so late, only hours before dawn."*

"No time to explain, just listen to me! You must move Shesha to a safer location, and take the eggs with you!"

"What?!" Duskeye's sleepiness vanished. *"What's happening?"*

Tallin heard the elves circle back. They were close, so close Tallin could hear their light-footed steps. Only seconds remained. "The elves are here, and they plan to steal Shesha's eggs! The elves are after me. Go south toward the desert—the tree sprites are spying for the elves, and the eggs won't be safe as long as you remain here. I can't talk anymore! Save the nest! Get Shesha out of this forest! Now!"

Duskeye tried to respond, but it was no use. Tallin's head felt like it was on fire. The buzzing in his ears was so loud now that it was intolerable. His concentration broke, and he lost contact.

Tallin jumped out of the tree hollow and dashed back among the trees. He scanned the area. Hiding in one spot wouldn't do him any good. They would find him eventually. If he avoided them long enough, maybe Duskeye could come and pick him up, but the safety of the eggs was the first priority. His only hope was to continue running, until he could get to a safer location. It wasn't the best plan, but it was the only one he had.

He could see Amandila in his peripheral vision; she was closing in on him from the side. A pool of dark water, smooth like a river stone, appeared in the distance. Tallin sprinted for the water. He would have to get across. It wasn't that wide, could he possibly jump over it? He wasn't sure. He pushed off on the mucky shore and leapt.

For a second, Tallin thought he was going to make it. Already planning his next steps, Tallin jerked his head down when he felt his feet brush the water. He had misjudged the distance.

He fell backwards into the pool, finding it deeper than he anticipated. The water rose up to his chest. He tried to swim up, but he couldn't move his feet. Mud sucked at his boots and up his legs until it reached his knees. His legs were stuck, and the more he struggled, the more he sank. Tallin tilted his head back and dirty water rushed into his nose.

Carnesîr's voice resonated in the distance. "Look over there! There he is!"

Tallin ducked down into the water, trying to pull his boots out of the mud, but his feet were stuck fast. He ducked under again, this time trying to remove his boots altogether, but it was already too late. When he came up to the surface for air, the elves were right behind him.

Sucking deep breaths, he heard the elves' footsteps as they approached. He was trapped like a fly in a spider's web.

"Strike him down, Amandila. But don't kill him." Carnesîr's voice was icy as he gave the order. Tallin tried to glance behind him, but a burst of searing light exploded in his face. Then something hard struck his temple. Red-hot fire erupted in his skull. His body stiffened, and Tallin collapsed into the brackish water.

His limbs felt hard and inflexible, like bars of iron that had been welded together. Tallin tried to speak, but only gurgling sounds came out. The only thing he could move was his eyes. When he looked up, he saw both elves standing over him. His head throbbed and it was painful even to breathe.

"I've got him," Amandila said. "Do you think he was able to warn anyone?" She dragged Tallin out of the water by his hair.

"I certainly hope not," Carnesîr replied. "But we'll know soon enough." He poked Tallin's side with his foot. "Is he still breathing?"

"Of course he's still breathing!" she said tartly. "What do you think? My aim is better than that."

She leaned over Tallin, touching him lightly on the forehead. "I only crippled him. It's temporary, but I'll have to carry him out."

With that, Amandila picked Tallin up and flung him over her shoulder, like a sack of turnips. Amandila was lithe and strong; she carried Tallin without assistance.

"Let's go. I'll question him back at our camp." They were still talking when Carnesîr waved his hand over Tallin's face. After that, the world went dark, and Tallin slept.

Skemtun and Kathir

I n the vast caverns of Mount Velik, Skemtun trudged back to his cave, bowed and bent, his knuckles throbbing after a long day's work. His back ached, and his mind felt like porridge. Sweat, gritty with dust, clung to his clothes and hair in a thick, uncomfortable layer of grime.

He was in a foul mood, and he hadn't had dinner yet, which made everything feel even worse. He'd spent the entire week mining copper ore with other members of his clan, *Marretaela.*

On top of his mining job, Skemtun was also a clan leader. While working in the mines sapped his physical energy, he found clan leadership even more tiring.

Last winter, Skemtun tried to resign from his position. Unfortunately, he found that resigning as a clan leader is something easier said than done. When he went to the council to submit his resignation, the group rebuked him and refused to grant his request. They said that, as clan leader, it was his responsibility to preserve the peace and to support his clan. Skemtun argued his case, but it did nothing to change their minds. The council's stone-like faces never budged. *He couldn't resign now,* they said, *not while the clans were still struggling. It would reflect poorly on the council.*

And so, Skemtun was forced to stay on. He was stuck. *I'm so tired—I'm tired of serving everybody around me. I want a change. I wish I could walk away from it all.*

Skemtun plodded along miserably. He felt broken down, physically and mentally. Toiling in the mines, his responsibilities to the council—it was so much work. Everything was too much.

Of course, the past few years had been hard on everyone. Times had changed, and not for the better. The dwarf clans always had disputes of one variety or another. But the problems had come to a head five years ago, when their king was nearly killed by an assassin.

After the attack, Hergung became bedridden. Once a great and powerful king, he was now weak and ineffectual. Without strong central leadership, the dwarves fell into embarrassing public squabbles, and a fierce power struggle erupted between the clans.

The first signs of serious trouble started with the Vardmiter clan. The Vardmiters got restless, and they didn't want to stay at Mount Velik. They became so displeased with the state of affairs that they abandoned

Mount Velik completely, moving west to the Highport Mountains. Their move had disastrous consequences for the other clans.

"Those lousy, rotten Vardmiters!" Skemtun swore under his breath. "They abandoned us when we needed them the most!"

Skemtun shook his fist in anger but then calmed himself down by taking a deep breath. The past was over and done... but not forgotten. No sense in brooding about it.

Skemtun thought of the last five years, going over the events in his mind. Trying to make sense of everything that happened. The Vardmiter clan was once the largest clan in Mount Velik; at one point, they had more clan members than all the other clans put together. And now they were gone. No clan had ever left Mount Velik before. With their move, the worst clan schism in their history had begun.

Skemtun sighed heavily. Perhaps they deserved this. Perhaps they should have known better.

A strict moral code had always dominated life in the dwarf kingdom, and the rules were oppressive to the lowest ranking clans. The Vardmiters were the lowest ranking clan in their social order, so they were often treated poorly. Other dwarves dismissed them. Mocked and belittled, the Vardmiters were treated more like animals than people.

The other clans didn't eat or drink with the Vardmiters, and they weren't invited to community events, not even ones in which all the other clans participated. They weren't allowed to marry outside their clan. The whole clan lived near the copper mines in deep, isolated caverns set in the bowels of Mount Velik.

It was rare that the Vardmiters had any physical contact with the other clans. Consequently, they couldn't move up the complex social hierarchy within the dwarf kingdom—their lives were set from birth.

The Vardmiters suffered through terrible working conditions and received unfairly low pay. But that was how it had been for thousands of years. It was tradition. And suddenly, the Vardmiters wanted to change all that. The Vardmiters' clan leader, Utan, was a passionate young upstart, committed to progressive change. Utan wanted to improve the living standards of his people.

Understandably, there was a lot of resistance to this type of radical change, especially from the other clans. During the early days leading up to the rebellion, Utan approached the dwarf council, asking for better working conditions and higher pay for his people. But his grievances were ignored, and the plight of the Vardmiters did not improve.

Utan became increasingly frustrated by the systematic denigration of his people, and he continued to fight for more rights. He complained directly to the king, but Hergung was very sick and could scarcely speak. Hergung deferred Utan back to the council, who dismissed his complaints yet again.

Infuriated, Utan began making secret plans to leave Mount Velik. He scouted for land and found a group of serviceable caves in the northwest region of the Highport Mountains. When Utan returned from his travels, he immediately called his clan together. On the day of the meeting, Utan stood in front of his clan and shouted, "We deserve better than this! The abuse of our people must stop! And it will! It stops today!"

With his passionate words, Utan whipped his clan into a frenzy. By the end of his speech, the Vardmiters were ready to follow him anywhere. And they did. The Vardmiters packed up and left Mount Velik under the cover of darkness that very same night, through a secret exit in the mountain. Their mass exodus was unlike anything the clans had ever seen.

Since no dwarf outside the Vardmiter clan ever entered their caves, news of the exodus didn't reach the other clans until the following morning, when gossip began spreading through the city like a prairie fire.

The other clans were incredulous. The dwarf council met and swiftly issued a formal pronouncement declaring it to be a temporary situation. The council maintained that the Vardmiters would return to Mount Velik in disgrace within days. A few council members even laughed about it. The council firmly believed that the Vardmiters would fail. They even started taking bets on when they would return. *No one should panic,* they insisted. *They'll come back soon enough.* Everyone calmed down a bit after that.

Too bad it was a lie. And Skemtun and the other dwarves had been foolish enough to believe it.

As the days turned into weeks, it became clear that the council was wrong.

Very wrong.

In desperation, the council sent spies to discover what the Vardmiters were doing. When the initial reports came back, the council refused to believe them.

The spies reported that the Vardmiters were doing well—thriving, in fact, in their new home. Although they had struggled at first, ultimately, they had persevered. Against all odds, the Vardmiters had succeeded.

On their own.

The Vardmiters weren't afraid to work hard to make their lives better. They pooled what little money they had and purchased three pigs; a boar and two sows. The pigs were easy to care for, because they could thrive on a diet of almost anything, including food scraps, acorns, and wild plants. From two breeding sows, the Vardmiters built their vast pig farms. All the female piglets were kept for breeding and the hogs fattened for consumption. They raised the pigs sensibly and treated them with care.

Under the Vardmiter's watchful husbandry, the sows multiplied by leaps and bounds, and within a year, the dwarves had a stable source of meat. In the meantime, women and children looked for food outside the mountain, gathering everything that was even remotely edible while they waited for their mushroom beds to mature. In this way, the Vardmiters survived their difficult first year.

After that, it only became easier for them.

As the conditions at Highport improved, the situation at Mount Velik deteriorated. No one was left to work the menial jobs that the Vardmiters used to do. The Vardmiters had performed all the unskilled jobs; they provided such vital services as garbage collection, sewage removal, general repairs, and burial of the dead.

The Vardmiters had also done most of the agricultural work, too, so their absence reduced the food supply. The citizens of Mount Velik tried to carry on as they did before, but it became impossible, and the kingdom tumbled into chaos.

Instead of conceding their mistakes and trying to set things right, the dwarf council argued even more. None of the clans wanted to do the lowly jobs the

Vardmiters used to do. They went back and forth for months as their society crumbled around them. Skemtun himself had argued against his clan picking up garbage, as it had seemed unthinkable at the time. With no one willing to step up, the catastrophe only worsened.

Near the caldera, where sunlight allowed some crops to grow, the abandoned fields became overgrown. Blight spread in the neglected soil, and all the crops perished. Their already limited farmland suffered great damage as a result. Drains became clogged and ceased to operate, and many caves were inundated with contaminated water.

The livestock went next. None of the higher clans wanted to touch farm animals. With no one to feed and care for them, all the chickens died. The rabbits went next.

Incredibly, their goat herds survived, but only because they were left outside to roam and graze; usually with no one attending them. When the Vardmiters left, they took their valuable sheep dogs with them, so many were killed by wolves. Some goats were even stolen by human farmers who lived in the valley below.

All the while, the dwarves' once-massive grain stores dwindled to nothing.

The population became desperate, which caused them to act recklessly. Outbreaks of violence occurred, and there was rioting inside the city. People fought, property was destroyed, and two dwarves were killed in the chaos. Only then did the council finally decide that the situation was critical. They were forced to admit the truth. The labor of the lowliest dwarf clan had been vital to the kingdom, and without the Vardmiters, their carefully structured society could not survive.

As riots consumed the city, the council swallowed their pride, and for the first time in recorded history assigned their clan members to menial work. Skemtun wasn't happy about it, no one was, but what else could they do?

The reassigned dwarves were skilled craftsmen who considered their new jobs incredibly demeaning. They complained bitterly about the physical labor, especially farming and cleaning, which the kingdom desperately needed to continue functioning.

After some negotiation, the clans forged a compromise. Every clan agreed to rotate their workers, with the majority of the extra labor coming from Marretaela, the mining clan, now the largest clan in the mountain. As Skemtun was leader of Marretaela, most of the additional labor fell to his people. He became responsible for delegating twice as much work as before. Skemtun had to push his clan members to take up where the Vardmiters left off.

The task was difficult, and it certainly wasn't pleasant. No one wanted to do all this extra work, but it was necessary. It was the only way to make the city function properly again. Eventually, his clan agreed to do as he said, but the new responsibilities were a constant burden, and the additional stress almost crippled him.

Finally, after several years, things were getting better. But nothing was as it had been before. Most dwarves worked two jobs. Everyone was exhausted. Women and children took over the cultivation and planting of the mushroom fields. And even with everyone working, it was still hard to get everything done.

There was simply too much work to be done. Old men and women, long retired, were forced back to work. Most worked unpaid, but they simply didn't have a choice. Everyone had to pitch in and help, or there wouldn't be enough for everyone to eat. And what would happen then?

Once the clans resigned themselves to their new roles, the situation at Mount Velik improved. They stripped out the diseased crops and replanted their fields with healthy plants. The new crops grew quickly now that they were being tended properly.

The dwarves succeeded in saving most of the goats. The goats were breeding again, so they had cheese and meat. And luckily, the orchards outside the mountain never stopped producing fruit.

A few more industrious dwarves managed to cultivate tracts of rye outside the mountain, so this year, they even had bread. Things were getting better. Slowly.

While they did have enough to eat these days, everything was still less plentiful than before, and food choices were limited. The days when one could choose between dozens of varied fruits and vegetables were over.

Skemtun glanced around him, knowing how bad things had gotten. They had simply ignored the problems for too long.

Why did we let it get this bad?

Skemtun shook his head as he passed through an empty corridor. It was a question he had no answer for. "If only we had fixed it sooner," Skemtun said under his breath. "It would 'ave been a lot less work for everybody."

He sighed. One step at a time.

Two young dwarves swung out into the corridor, chatting and laughing. Gazing down at his feet, Skemtun didn't even notice until they bumped into him.

"Whoops! Sorry, old man," one said. "I didn't see ye there."

Skemtun looked up and saw a familiar face. It belonged to his cousin, Garaek, the youngest son of his sister Marna. If he remembered correctly, Garaek had just turned thirty this year. "That's all right, son," Skemtun replied. "Where ye lads headed?"

"To the mead hall!" the other one said, clapping Skemtun so hard on the back that he sputtered. "We need a stiff drink an' a hot meal. Ye should join us!" They laughed and carried on their way.

Skemtun's face lifted. *What a great idea! A break is what I need.* If there was one thing he wanted, it was a good meal in the company of friends.

He changed direction and hurried down the corridor that led to the mead hall. The hall was positioned at the end of the market, and since it was market day, all the tables were full.

Fruits and vegetables, mushrooms and meat; the tables were piled high, though not as high as they once had been. Skemtun could remember the days when sellers would simply give away the older produce. But now, even rotting vegetables, overripe fruit, and green-tinged meat were all sold and used for something.

He paused at the entrance and scanned the huge room. The hall was filled to capacity and bustled with activity. The Vardmiters weren't allowed here anymore, but dwarves from every other clan walked around, chatting and doing business. Old dwarves played cards near the fireplace, and children played up and down the aisles. There were a few humans, too, merchants from the outside.

It was a communal gathering place—a cafeteria, meeting room, and a recreation space all in one. Skemtun squeezed through a large group of stonecutters and went inside.

Torchlight reflected off the ornate metalwork on the tables and chairs. Iron spears and animal skins hung on the walls. The scents of ale and cooking food filled the air, making his stomach rumble. He passed by other dwarves in his clan, waving and saying hello. Sometimes he stopped to talk, but he tried to keep the conversations short.

The more he smelled food, the more he wanted it. Pushing through the crowds, Skemtun found a seat at a smaller table near the kitchen. He caught the eye of a serving girl and motioned with his finger. The young woman stopped wiping tables and walked over to him.

"Hello, Skemtun. Haven't seen ye in a while." she said with a smile.

"I've been busy, ye know," he replied.

"Haven't we all? Now then, what'll ye be havin' today?"

He thought for a moment, looking at the giant painted menu above the kitchen doors. "I'll 'ave a goat platter with mushrooms. Do ye have any bread today?"

She shook her head. "Nay, not today. There's no flour until next week."

"Too bad. How 'bout one o' those fancy honey cakes?" he asked. "I'd like one o' those."

"Aye, we do 'ave a few. Will half of one be enough? The king likes 'em, so we're tryin' to ration 'em a bit."

"That's fine. I'll take whatever ye can give me. And bring me a big jug o' ale from the cellar." He dug into his pocket and tossed her a copper coin. The girl caught it in the air with her free hand. With a small smile on her lips, she tucked the coin into her apron. "Thank ye, sir. I'll be right back with yer plate." She spun around and disappeared into the kitchen.

Skemtun leaned back and let his mind relax while he waited for his order. All around him, people chatted and laughed. A rousing song erupted at a nearby table, and an enthusiastic group jumped up to sing, swaying back and forth as they loudly shouted the lyrics.

Skemtun smiled and began to whistle. It was an old melody, a bard's tribute to a lost love. He'd heard this song a thousand times before.

More and more stood up to sing, and some even leapt on top of their tables. Soon, the whole place was singing along.

I see the face of my fair maiden,

In the stars each night up high,

Her eyes they haunt me still,

T'was just three moons ago she died,

I held 'er near, and I held 'er tight,

That blessed day, I swore I'd love 'er all me life.

But she was lost to me one summer night,

Aye, ohhh ...those stormy winds shall blow.

He felt tears welling up in his eyes and rubbed them away. The serving girl reappeared minutes later with a heaping tray of meat and mushrooms, still steaming from the ovens. The food was a welcome sight.

She placed the plate in front of him along with a jug of ale. Skemtun rubbed his hands together, sniffing the delicious aroma. "Thank ye, lass, this looks delicious. It's fine and warm."

He yanked the stopper off the jug and took a long drink. The cold ale went down his throat in a frothy torrent. "By Golka, that tastes good," he said, wiping foam from his beard with the back of his hand.

"Och! Ye're sure enjoyin' it! Ye must 'ave been thirsty!" the girl teased him.

"Aye," he said, nodding. "I always enjoy good food and drink, 'specially if I don't 'ave to cook it!"

She offered him another smile. "Will that be all now?"

"Just keep the drinks comin', lass," Skemtun said. "As soon as you see I'm gettin' empty, bring me another round."

She nodded. "All right then, enjoy yer supper," she said as she walked away, moving on to the next hungry customer.

He pulled a sharp little knife from his waistband and wiped it on his sleeve. Then he sliced a corner of fat, swirled it in gravy and took a bite. The first taste was so good that he barely paused to chew.

He carved more meat and popped it in his mouth, relishing the way the fatty bits melted with the saucy mushrooms in his mouth. Juices dribbled down his chin. He wiped them off with his hand, not stopping for a moment. With every swallow, he felt better.

Silently, he finished off the last of the meat, washed it down with beer, and pushed his empty plate away. He felt much better after the meal—at peace somehow. Skemtun started humming a happy tune.

It was then that he realized someone was watching him. He scanned the shadiest corners of the hall, squinting into the hazy darkness. In a corner near the fireplace, he spotted a tall human man. Skemtun ventured a quick glance at the stranger. He stood with shoulders squared and hands behind him, his face shadowed by the flickering torch on the wall.

They locked eyes for a few seconds before Skemtun snapped his head away. He didn't have the energy to deal with any humans right now.

The man walked straight toward him. Skemtun held his breath. *What does this person want?* The man stepped closer and closer, and Skemtun hoped he would walk right past him as if he weren't there. Humans always brought problems.

But he didn't pass by. Instead, the stranger stopped right behind Skemtun and tapped him on the shoulder. "Pardon," he said. "Sorry to interrupt your meal, but I've got to speak with you. Where can we talk?"

Skemtun turned to study the man's shadowed profile. The stranger wore a thick cloak with a hood drawn down, slightly covering his face. He was tall, with curly dark hair visible at his neckline. Skemtun frowned. He *really* didn't need this today. It was hard enough dealing with his job and coming off a long shift. But he decided to be polite. "Well, neighbor, you're welcome to pull up a stool and have a seat." Skemtun's voice rose slightly as he spoke.

"Not here, if you please. Let's speak in private." The lines around the stranger's mouth grew deeper. His expression was serious.

Skemtun eyed the man. A few tense moments passed. "So… do I know ye?" he asked, examining the man's face. He didn't look familiar.

"No, I don't believe we've met before."

Skemtun shifted in his seat. The man had the dark skin of a gypsy peddler. That wasn't uncommon around these parts. Gypsy merchants came through the dwarf kingdom quite frequently hoping to trade their goods. "Are ye a merchant?" he asked, tilting his head to the side. "Because ye're not allowed t' solicit here. The merchant rules are strict—they're posted right outside the doors. If ye'd like to inquire about metal tradin', ye'll have to make an appointment with me durin' the day."

The man shook his head. "Look, mate …I'm not trying to sell you anything. I just want to talk."

Skemtun's eyebrows crept up. "About what?" his hands fidgeted nervously with his knife. The way the man stood, towering over him, gave Skemtun a queasy feeling.

"I can't go into details, but it's very important that we speak."

Skemtun feigned disinterest and tried to dismiss the stranger with a wave of his hand. "Look, I'm sure this can wait until tomorrow. I was just startin' to enjoy my evenin' meal, and now ye've spoilt it. Just leave... *please.* I want to be alone."

The stranger said nothing, but Skemtun could feel his glare.

The man folded his arms and didn't move. "I've traveled a long way, *Skemtun Shalecarver!* Even if we have to sit here all night, I'm not leaving until you speak with me." The stranger leaned down, cupping his hand over Skemtun's ear.

The dwarf's back stiffened, but he didn't move. The man whispered, "The wizards of the Crystal City sent me."

Skemtun's jaw dropped open, and he spun around in his seat. "*Miklagard* sent you? The High Council of Miklagard?"

"Ssshh! Keep your bloody voice down, will you?" The stranger hissed, glancing nervously around the room. He grabbed Skemtun's shoulder and pulled him up from his seat.

His previous weariness forgotten, Skemtun replied in a hoarse whisper, "Okay, okay…come with me."

As Skemtun walked out to leave, a cry of protest rose from the other tables, one dwarf shouting, "Hey! Where ye goin', Skemtun? Don't leave yet!"

Another dwarf yelled, "Aye, the party's just begun! Don't be a wet blanket, old man! Stay a while longer."

Skemtun opened his mouth to reply, but then thought better of it. If he tried to argue, his friends would only try harder to convince him to stay. And that was mighty tempting, even with this potentially serious matter on his hands.

He ignored them and scurried out of the hall. The stranger followed him out. Skemtun looked around to make sure no one was following them, and then took a sharp turn into a dark corridor. They traveled down the passage and up a set of winding stone stairs before turning into a short causeway. After crossing over a large metal pipe, they stopped outside a dark, narrow tunnel.

Skemtun paused to light a stub of candle. "It's always dark up here; there's no torches in this area."

The tunnel was only a few spans wide, and the stranger had to walk sideways like a crab in order to move through it. At the end of the passage was a much larger cave, filled to the ceiling with empty crates. "We used to store grain in here," Skemtun said, "but all our stores are gone. Lately, there hasn't been any extra to store."

They walked up a short row of steps that led to a small cave. The entrance was decorated with polished stones, each a different size and shade. Small runes were engraved onto their surfaces.

Skemtun drew back an animal skin that covered the opening. "We'll talk in here," he said, motioning toward the room. Skemtun could still hear a faint sound of music drifting up from the hall as they stepped inside.

It was a small space, filled with moldy-smelling air. "Wait a second, I'll light this lamp." Skemtun went over to the table and picked up a dusty globe filled with an oily yellow liquid. He touched the candle flame to a charred wick inside. There was a flash. The flame sputtered and then steadied. Skemtun adjusted the wick until it burned as brightly as it would without smoking.

The man released the cover back over the entrance and stepped inside. "Is it safe to talk in here?" he asked, surveying the room. The dim flame revealed four stools and a simple stone table. A dirty rope hung on the wall, but there wasn't much else.

"As safe as anywhere in this mountain," replied Skemtun, nodding toward the walls. "There's spies everywhere."

They sat down at the table. The stranger flipped his hood back and leaned into the flickering light of the oil lamp, revealing deep marks on both cheeks. Calm gray eyes gazed steadily at him. He folded his hands in front of him and waited.

Skemtun pointed at the man's face. "Those scars on yer cheeks; I've seen 'em before. A slaver's knife made those, right? Now I'm *sure* we've never met before. I would've remembered those scars."

The stranger nodded slowly. "Yes. They're flesh merchant's scars. I was slave, once. I was kidnapped by slavers when I was a child. I escaped my masters when I was a teenager."

Skemtun looked surprised. "How did ye escape? Slavers are usually pretty nasty."

The man looked away. It was obvious he didn't want to talk about it. "I was lucky. I was beaten daily, treated like an animal. Finally, I could stand it no more. I stole money from my master and ran into the desert." He finished softly, "That's all in the past. A lifetime ago."

Skemtun looked pensive for a second before he blurted out, "So, now that you're here, who are ye? And what do ye want from me?"

"My name is Kathir. I'm a mercenary ...of sorts. A soldier for hire. I've been working for Miklagard for several years." He stretched his collar open, revealing a neck free of tattoos. "I'm not an outlander, though. Don't lump me in with bounty hunter filth."

Skemtun calmed down a little. Now he was more curious than afraid. "Who sent ye? And why are ye here? But don't lie. Ye can't trick me. I'm good at readin' people."

"I wasn't lying when I told you why I've come here. The wizards of the Crystal City hired me to come here and meet you. Miklagard is quite concerned about your welfare and safety."

Skemtun shook his head. *It didn't make any sense.* "But why? What could the High Council want with me? I've never even spoken to them, except maybe in passing."

"You and Bolrakei are the only surviving clan leaders in Mount Velik. Your king is on the edge of death. Miklagard believes that your life is important enough to safeguard, so they sent me here to protect you, and also to give you a warning to share with your people."

Skemtun scoffed. "King Hergung is sick, but he's not dyin' yet. And I can take care o' myself. I'm a decent fighter."

Kathir smiled, his thin lips twitching. "Calm yourself, Skemtun. I meant no insult. Your king's worsening health isn't even the worst news. There's more. A military threat has crystallized against you in the west. The orcs plan to assault Mount Velik before winter. The orc king greatly desires this territory for himself. If the greenskins start their war march now, they'll catch you unprepared. The orcs will destroy your people. And this isn't like before. There will be more orcs in this army than you can possibly imagine."

Skemtun shrugged. "Aye, I've heard a few rumors, but nothin' that serious."

Kathir's expression turned sour. "They're not just rumors! The danger is real, and it's close upon you. The orcs are definitely planning an attack."

"Do you have any proof? Who's your source for this information?"

"Miklagard assured me that the intelligence was reliable," said Kathir.

Skemtun leaned back and touched the fingertips of his hands together in front of his face. "I need more proof than *that* if I'm going to go to the dwarf council with this story. I can't cause an uproar on your word alone. I don't even know ye!"

"You can't just sit back and do nothing. You must warn the other clans. The dwarf council doesn't listen to outsiders. They won't take any advice from me, or from the Crystal City. I know that much. You're a clan leader, so it's your job to be responsible, at least for the sake of your own people."

Skemtun spread his hands. "Well, what can I do? I'm just one man. I'm not even a soldier, I'm a miner. Why would they listen to me?"

"You have influence. You can still warn the council, and you can tell your people to prepare for war."

Skemtun balked. "Prepare for war? On the basis of a *rumor?* I can't do that! It'll cause a panic, especially after everything that's happened."

"You're just being stubborn. Or perhaps you're afraid. A timely warning could save this mountain. Think of your people."

Skemtun squirmed in his seat. "Look, I understand there's some danger. But I can't just stick my neck out like that. If I go to the council talking about threats of war without any proof, then they'll think I'm crazy! They don't want to hear about distant threats. The council doesn't take me seriously. They don't listen to me. They just tell me what to do. Besides, they're too busy arguin' over the Vardmiter revolt. The whole council is still pretty upset about that."

"These are *not* distant threats. Nothing is more important than what I'm telling you now," Kathir said wearily. "Your council must take heed. War with the orcs is imminent."

Skemtun raised his hand. "I disagree. If the orcs aren't actually marchin' in our direction, then I think such talk is a *wee bit* premature. Ye've got to understand how things work around here. It's not like the human realm. Dwarves don't make quick decisions like that, even when the whole world wants us to. We like to *deliberate* on things."

"Deliberate faster. By the time the orcs start their march, it will be too late for you to prepare." Kathir said.

Skemtun shook his head. "The orcs have always been a threat to us, and they always will be. If they attack, we'll find a way to get through it, same as we always have." Skemtun wasn't about to budge, especially over some rumors from a human stranger.

Kathir paused and decided to take another approach. "You're not being completely truthful with yourself, are you? Things are very different than they were in the past."

Skemtun stiffened in his seat.

Kathir could tell he had hit a nerve, and continued. "Life at Mount Velik is more precarious now, isn't it? Your population has been cut in half. When the Vardmiters left, they took all their able-bodied men with them. How are you going to fight the orc armies with only half your men? You'll be totally unprepared."

Skemtun snorted. "Bah! The Vardmiters! We don't need *them* to beat a few greenskins. We're gettin' along fine without those buggers!"

Kathir kept pressing. "If you're getting along fine without the Vardmiters, then why grow so angry at the mere mention of them?"

Skemtun huffed and crossed his arms. "I'm not! We're makin' do. Besides, those turncoats wouldn't be any help to us anyhow. They can't fight worth a damn."

"Are you so sure about that? Your leadership has consistently underestimated the strength and resilience of the Vardmiters. You seem to believe that simply because you have a few skilled warriors, you'll be victorious. If war comes to your front gate, Mount Velik will be at a considerable disadvantage without their manpower."

"Nay, that's a load of rubbish! The Vardmiters don't have any proper fighters. We have lots of trained soldiers. Lots! They don't! I'm tellin' ye—we don't *need* the Vardmiters. We're doing fine without 'em."

"That's not true. The Vardmiters might lack resources, but they're very industrious and capable of surviving tough conditions. Mount Velik is at a considerable disadvantage without them. I mean...don't they even have their own spellcaster now? One that serves them willingly?"

Another pause. Skemtun coughed and cleared his throat. "Well ...yes," he admitted. "They do have *one* spellcaster. Name's Mugla. But she's very old. Probably even senile. But enough about that! I don't want to talk about them anymore. They're a bunch of traitors."

"Not everyone believes that, you know. I went to Highport recently. Utan described how horribly they were treated here. Is it any wonder they left?"

Skemtun frowned and bit his lip. He *really* didn't want to talk about this, but he managed to subdue his rising anger and tried to change the subject again. "If the orcs attack us, we'll defend the mountain. Our clans are strong. We have enough warriors to fight the greenskins."

Kathir lowered his voice. "Having trained warriors isn't enough. Your clans have a bigger problem than the threat of war, and that is one of internal conflict. How can you defend your kingdom against an outside attack with so much civil unrest within? The division between the dwarf clans places the security of the entire eastern seaboard at risk. That's why I was sent here—to warn you and the other clan leaders."

"We're strong enough to defeat the orcs," Skemtun insisted again, keeping his arms locked against his chest. "We have enough men."

"Perhaps. Perhaps not. What if another clan decides to leave Mount Velik as the Vardmiters did? The remaining clans won't be strong enough to defend this mountain against any outside attack, much less the orcs. The dwarf clans are more vulnerable now than they've been in centuries."

"Look, I still don't see how our problems affect Miklagard. What do the white wizards care about dwarf politics?"

Kathir sighed and rolled his eyes. "Can you really not see it? Everyone else can. The orcs are multiplying like rabbits. In the past, the orcs kept their own population in check by participating in vicious death-battles, but King Nar has outlawed them. Their numbers have exploded, and they're looking for new lands to conquer. The orcs are testing the boundaries of their territory. The dragon riders killed several small bands attempting to cross the northern border of the desert. They're ready for war. If Mount Velik falls to the greenskins, then the orcs will have a stable foothold in the east. If they capture Mount Velik, they'll control the east and the northwest. Once that happens, they'll march on the capital city. Morholt is heavily fortified, but there's no way the city could stand the onslaught of two huge orc armies. And, if Morholt is conquered, it's only a matter of time before Parthos falls too. The orcs could overtake the entire continent in a decade. But in order to do that, they need to conquer Mount Velik first, and they know it."

Skemtun exhaled and shrunk back on his stool. The horrible possibility became clear under Kathir's waiting gaze. For the first time since they had started talking, Skemtun felt nauseated. "Maybe you do have a point."

"Yes," Kathir said, nodding, "I do. This is a very credible threat. The orcs have always desired this mountain, but their previous leaders have been either too bloodthirsty or too stupid to lead the orc armies to victory. King Nar is different. He's intelligent and calculating. That's bad news for the rest of the mortal races, but it's especially terrible for yours."

Skemtun threw up his hands. "All right! I'll admit things are bad. But what can I do? How can I convince the council?"

"Start by talking to them. Stay positive, but warn them of the danger. Miklagard hopes you'll be the voice of reason; that you'll take this critical information to your leadership, and they'll act on it, before it's too late."

"But why me?" Skemtun's voice was full of anxiety.

"We came to you first, because there was *no one else* to turn to. Utan left with his Vardmiters, and Bolrakei cares about no one but herself. Hergung is too sick to do anything, much less lead your clans into battle. Who else could we trust with this information? Do you understand now?"

Skemtun's lip trembled. He looked defeated. "Aye," he said softly. "I do. I'll talk to the other families. Maybe they'll listen to me," he concluded lamely.

"That's our hope. Miklagard has been quietly observing the situation at Mount Velik for a long time. Hergung is in terrible health and has no legitimate successor. Once he dies, the clans will be united under a new ruler. Miklagard favors *you* for kingship."

Skemtun gave a bitter shout of laughter. "Ha! That's not going to happen. Bolrakei is well-loved among the clans, and she's itchin' to be queen. That greedy witch is number one in line, ye can bet on it."

Kathir crossed his arms and shook his head. "You're wrong. Bolrakei is too power hungry and irresponsible to be queen. She cares nothing for the welfare of her people unless it fattens her own coffers. It's not as if this is a big secret, Skemtun."

"We don't have to worry about that for a while yet. King Hergung might be in poor health, but as long as he's living, he's still my king. Hergung's got a few good summers left in him."

Kathir said calmly, "Do you really believe that? Is that what the king's physicians have been telling you? That Hergung has a lot of time left?"

"Yes. Why? What do *you* say?" Skemtun asked, leaning forward.

"Miklagard has more accurate information than you, it seems. They have their own spies here, as you probably guessed."

A bewildered worry flitted across the dwarf's brow. "I guess that's no surprise. Everyone seems to wants to stick their nose in our business. That's why the dwarf council doesn't like outsiders. They're always meddling in our affairs. The humans, the elves, even the Balborites! The Balborite assassin that attacked our king five years ago almost killed him, but Hergung pulled through. I'm lucky to be alive myself."

"Speaking of that...two other clan leaders were killed that day. Why haven't the clans elected new leaders to replace the ones that were killed? It's been five years already."

Skemtun shrugged. "Lots o' reasons, I guess. Five years isn't a long time for us. Dwarves are a long-lived people. The clans aren't stupid. Everybody knows that Hergung is really sick, and they're waitin' before they elect new leaders. A clan leader serves for hundreds of years. We like to be sure about our leadership choices."

"Well, you'll be choosing new clan leaders soon, as well as your new king. That time is closer than you think. Your life is also in danger. As soon as Hergung dies, Bolrakei will try to kill you. You're right to think she wants to be queen. She wants it so badly that she won't risk you'll be chosen as the new king, even if the possibility is small."

Skemtun laughed bitterly. "That ain't news to me, stranger. Bolrakei's threatened me plenty of times already. She hates me and wants me gone."

There was a long stretch of silence where neither said anything. Skemtun licked his lips and looked across the table. "Maybe your spies are wrong? The council says the king will survive another year. So maybe they're exaggerating, and he's only got a few more months."

Kathir shook his head. "No. The situation is worse than that. Hergung is already on his deathbed. He shall not live to see the next full moon. King Hergung has only days to live. That's why I was sent out here so quickly."

The dwarf let out a nervous laugh. "Come, come, now. I've had enough scares for tonight. He's got a few seasons, a few months, maybe. Not days. It's impossible he's that sick."

Kathir shook his head. "How would you know? Have you seen him lately?"

Skemtun face fell. "Well, no, but..."

"Your king cannot eat, walk, or even talk anymore. He's past the point of no return. There's nothing the doctors can do for him. Things in this kingdom are about to change, and quicker than you think."

And then, as if on cue, the clang of a gong resonated through the air, cutting through the silence like a knife. The gong sounded again, deeper and louder than before. The mountain stilled.

"No!" gasped Skemtun, the blood draining from his face. "It can't be! Not this soon!"

"I'm afraid so," Kathir said.

The gong sounded a third and final time. Everyone knew what it meant. It was the death gong, the official announcement that the dwarf king had died. There was nothing more to say.

Skemtun buried his face in his hands. He shuddered, his chin quivering. "Nay, nay…" Fat tears rolled down his cheeks and into his beard.

A great lamentation rose up inside the mountain. The sound went through the caverns, creeping upward like a giant wave.

Kathir placed his hand on the old dwarf's trembling shoulder. "I'm very sorry. I know you didn't expect it to happen so soon, but your king is dead. The clans must now choose his successor. Until they do, you'll be in constant danger. It looks like I won't be leaving Mount Velik after all. I shall remain here to protect you. I'm your new bodyguard."

A Funeral Interrupted

The oxen were chosen, the food prepared, and the funeral litter decorated with thousands of flowers. Everyone prepared for the funeral. The bird messengers went out five days earlier, a steady stream of foreign visitors had been arriving since then. Mount Velik had become increasingly crowded, and now all the caverns were full. Any new visitors were forced to stay outside in tents.

The king's body had been preserved by dwarf spellcasters and was laid out in a private chamber. It seemed especially quiet in the mountain, with all the normal sounds of a bustling city subdued. The funeral would be held this evening, and Skemtun and Kathir were getting dressed.

Skemtun washed his hair and curled his long beard with heated metal rollers. Then he put on a long gray tunic and strapped an ornate belt around his waist. Kathir dressed himself in a long-sleeved black shirt and heavy trousers. He and Skemtun cleaned and shined their boots in silence.

Skemtun nodded to Kathir. "Best we go now. It's about time we left. Gettin' tired of watchin' these foreigners come and go anyhow."

Kathir nodded back, and they left the upper caverns, walking down to the main gate where the funeral march would begin. They secured a place in the front of the line, right by the entrance. Low drums sounded. The sound of ox hoofs reached their ears, accompanied by soft voices and quiet weeping.

The crowd was getting larger now. The king's funeral procession came near; the line of mourners stretched back as far as the eye could see, forming a long gray queue that snaked through the corridors. The line moved slowly, like molasses dripping from a pipe.

Kathir whispered into Skemtun's ear. "Who will lead the procession? You or Bolrakei?"

"We're both allowed to walk up front with our clan flags. The other clans chose people to represent them, but they've got to walk in the back, because they don't have official clan leaders right now. Now that Hergung has died, things will change. After the funeral is over, a new king will be chosen, and the other clans will elect new leaders, too."

For once, the dwarves' circular logic made sense to him. Then a thought came to him. "Didn't Hergung have a son? Whatever happened to him?"

Skemtun nodded. "He's too young to take the throne. The boy's barely fifty years of age. He's naught but a baby in dwarf years. If he'd been older, he would've been considered for the position. But the clans can't wait another fifty years to elect a king. The clans will nominate a new king from the highest ranking members in the clans. Only dwarves from the best families will be considered."

"The highest-ranking dwarves? So is Bolrakei going to be nominated?"

Skemtun didn't want to admit it, but he knew it was true. "Yes... she is high born. Her blood is pure. So she's a top candidate. She wants to be queen."

"What about the Vardmiters? Are they invited to the funeral?"

"No," Skemtun said, his voice irritated. "Why do ye have to bring them into this, especially today? They aren't welcome at Mount Velik anymore."

But Kathir wouldn't let the issue go. "But why? Wasn't Hergung their king, too?"

Skemtun looked pained. "Look, I don't want to talk about them right now. After everything that's happened, they shouldn't come here, especially not now, while everyone's upset."

"What happens if a few of them show up?"

Now Skemtun looked smug. "Ha! They already did. The Vardmiters sent two raggedy emissaries here yesterday. The guards recognized them right away, with all their freckles and red hair. They arrived on a donkey, holding a silly gift and some paper flowers. The guards set them straight pretty quickly. They were given a sound drubbing and thrown out."

Kathir raised an eyebrow at him. "You beat them, simply because they showed up and tried to pay their respects? You punished them because of that?"

Another silence followed this, but Skemtun was anxious and he broke it. "Well, of *course* it sounds bad when ye put it that way."

Kathir spoke. "It sounds bad whichever way you put it. You've all acted terribly in this case. The Vardmiters have a right to be here. Hergung was their leader, too. Everyone deserves a second chance. I should know."

Skemtun didn't expect to feel guilty, but Kathir's accusing words drilled into him. Maybe the Vardmiters didn't deserve what happened. But, still...they'd left! Despite his tangled emotions, he smiled. "Look, maybe ye're right, and we can make amends with them someday. But not right now; there's still too much resentment."

Kathir nodded and let the issue drop.

Several mourners stepped into the main walkway and started dropping flower petals near the doors. A ceremonial circle had been etched into the floor using brightly colored chalk. There was a carved statue of the king in the center of the circle. The statue showed a robed Hergung sitting on an ornate bronze throne, happy and smiling, looking up into the heavens. The likeness was incredible.

Skemtun marveled at how quickly the statue had been carved. Or perhaps it had been created years before in anticipation of this day. Kathir reached out to touch it, and Skemtun slapped his hand away with a grimace. "Nobody touches the statue until the end!" he scolded softly.

Clad in white, ten sharply dressed attendants gathered near the doors. They wore pointed hats secured to their heads with silver thread. A bell sounded from far away, and the attendants scurried off, disappearing into an upper chamber.

In the background, the funeral band played on. A mournful ballad rose through the caverns, drowning out everything else.

As if on cue, Bolrakei entered a side corridor, surrounded by her advisors. She was a sight to behold. She had refused to wear the official colors of mourning. Instead of gray or white, her vast bulk was squeezed into a shiny green dress, topped with a metallic cape.

The whole outfit was decorated with peacock feathers. Her neck and wrists glittered with jewels. To complete the ensemble, she had chosen an enormous plumed headdress, which trailed silver ribbons that reached down to her waist.

It was the gaudiest attire that Skemtun had ever seen, especially at a funeral. But no one said anything out loud. Skemtun just shook his head. It wouldn't be right to curse at a funeral.

A single trumpet sounded, and the band went silent.

The attendants walked down the stairs, carrying the funeral litter into the waiting crowd below. Everyone could see the body clearly; the king's hands were folded, and his expression was peaceful. The spellcasters had done an excellent job covering the king's scars and mottled skin. He looked like a younger version of himself, and it was as if he were merely sleeping.

Everyone waved their clan flags and stood aside while the two clan leaders positioned themselves at the front. Bolrakei and Skemtun stood side-by-side, not arguing for once. Theirs were places of honor. Skemtun glanced into the crowd. Kathir kept a respectful distance, but he was still in sight. Four other dwarves stepped forward to represent the remaining clans, but they stayed in the back, behind the king.

Skemtun raised his clan flag and stepped forward. The main gates were opened, and the king's body was carried outside where it was immediately lowered to the ground for a prayer. He shot a disgusted look at Bolrakei, who was waving enthusiastically, as if she were in a carnival procession.

He realized then how glad he was to have Kathir with him. The man's constant presence had taken some getting used to, but Skemtun was thankful for the extra protection. *Especially with this overgrown peacock strutting around!*

The chief spellcaster, a withered old dwarf in a black robe, approached the body, chanting loudly in an ancient language. His mouth was drawn in a somber frown. Skemtun recognized a few words here and there, but otherwise he couldn't understand what was being said. *It's nothin' but old wizard chatter anyway.*

The crowd hushed as the wizard drew a small statuette from his robe. It started to glow, and the wizard placed it between Hergung's clasped hands. The old spellcaster knelt over the body and pressed two fingers to the king's forehead. A smear of ash remained where the spellcaster had touched the king's face. The old mage said a final prayer and tossed a handful of dirt onto the litter. It disappeared among the flowers and other offerings.

Carrying a bronze censer filled with incense, the mage went three times around the litter. Then, he stepped back and raised his hands to the heavens, his long robes swaying back and forth. "Return to the earth, dear king! Descend to your final sleep with my benediction upon your name! Farewell! Farewell!" he chanted.

"Farewell! Farewell!" The crowd repeated.

"May ye rest in peace for all eternity," said the mage.

Once again, the crowd repeated, "For all eternity! Oh, for all eternity!"

The incense smelled strongly of medicinal herbs, and the fragrant smoke masked any odor from the body. The sun was high in the sky by the time the litter was placed on its carriage and hitched to the oxen. The carriage attendants settled into their positions, holding willow switches to spur the oxen.

The official procession began in the afternoon, in the orchards outside the gates. Slowly, the crowd lurched forward in its ritual march. Skemtun led the column, with Bolrakei at his side. Again he wished someone else were there standing next to him—anyone but her. He glanced back. Hundreds of dwarves followed behind, praying, singing, and crying as they went.

Skemtun breathed deeply. The air from the surrounding forest was warm and carried a soft perfume from blooming flowers. There weren't any clouds in the sky, so it was hot, and Skemtun was wearing thick clothing. Compared to the relative cool of the dwarf caverns, it felt unpleasantly warm outside.

Skemtun pulled a handkerchief from his pocket and wiped the sweat off his brow. He hoped the procession would move faster. The prayers had taken a long time. If they stayed out in this heat much longer, they might need to hold a few more funerals. He wasn't the only one who was uncomfortable, either.

Sweat trickled from the brows of many of the mourners. Fanning her chubby face with her hand, Bolrakei looked ready to collapse.

There were thousands of willow buds floating in the air. It seemed like an odd time of year for it, so Skemtun couldn't tell if the falling blossoms were natural or something that the spellcasters had added to the ceremony. The tiny white buds made many of the dwarves sneeze as they fell like snow upon the crowd.

The mourners made their way up the rocky track that circled the mountain. Skemtun huffed, sweating more profusely as they began their steady climb up the mountainside. The procession would climb upward toward the caldera; the trek would take several hours and would end at sunset. A double row of oil torches lined the edges of the path. The torches would be lit after sundown, when the procession made its way back down the mountain.

Skemtun walked on. The trail began to get rougher, and he noticed that people were starting to stumble. Everyone was hot and tired. As they ascended higher up the mountain, the path was partially broken away, and people had to squish together to pass. Debris from the mountain-side collected at the shoulder, narrowing the path. The march slowed.

Bolrakei started to curse under her breath.

There were holes and missing pavestones everywhere. The road was overgrown with weeds in some places. In the worst spots, a wood panel had to be placed underneath the carriage wheels so the wagon could continue moving forward. The roads had been neglected and had become more and more dangerous with time, but the problem had been relatively easy to ignore ...until now.

It was another reminder of the work that was left undone after the Vardmiters left. They were the road builders, and maintenance was neglected now that they were gone. The procession moved slower and slower until finally the carriage came to a dead stop, unable to move because of a boulder that had materialized in the middle of the path.

The attendants hurried up the trail, looking for a way around the obstacle.

But that wasn't enough for Bolrakei, who was by now completely incensed. She shouted and cursed.

"Why wasn't this road cleared before the procession began?"

Skemtun tried to ignore her outburst. This was a funeral, after all. It wasn't an appropriate place for a squabble. But soon other dwarves began arguing as well.

Somehow it exploded into a shouting match of escalating curses. The band stopped playing. Children were screaming, irritated by the heat and the noise.

Skemtun looked back and locked eyes with Kathir, who was standing several steps behind him in the crowd. They were both thinking the same thing. The ceremony was a disaster. A funeral shouldn't be like this. *If this goes on much longer, there's going to be a riot.*

Bolrakei kept screaming, "Why wasn't this taken care of yesterday? How are we supposed to move forward? This is outrageous!" Then she pointed an accusing finger at Skemtun. "*You* should have fixed this!"

"It's not *my* responsibility to clean up the roads!" Skemtun said angrily.

"Then whose responsibility is it?" she screeched back. "No one ever told *me* that the roads needed clearing."

"That's a good question," Skemtun said, his voice dripping with sarcasm. "Maybe you should clean them up? Yer clan is the *laziest* in the entire kingdom!"

Bolrakei gasped with fury. *"What* did you say to me? How dare you insult me in this manner!" She flung her head back, and in the process lost her fancy hat. It tumbled off her head and became a tangled mess of tassels and plucked feathers on the ground. Skemtun tried to calm the crowd while Bolrakei raged on about her ruined headdress.

Just then, a lightning flash burst in the sky. Skemtun blinked, looked up, and placed his hand over his eyes. A deafening roar shook the earth beneath them. People dropped to the ground and covered their heads. When Skemtun glanced up, he saw what had made the noise. An enormous white dragon circled overhead, the largest he had ever seen. The crowd gasped.

Another dragon joined the first, a smaller female with scars on both wings. Both of the dragons had riders. It was Sela, the leader of the dragon riders, along with her carnelian dragon, Brinsop. Elias rode his colossal white dragon, Nydeired.

The white dragon descended slowly. His wings were so large that it looked like he was flying in slow motion. There was no space for Nydeired to land on the path, so he flew a short distance up the mountain and landed there. When the white dragon's feet touched down, the ground trembled.

Brinsop flew down and landed closer to the crowd. Sela jumped off her dragon's back and approached the dwarves.

Bolrakei smoothed her expression and adopted a frozen grin. "Why, hello, Sela! Thank you for attending the funeral. We appreciate your presence during this difficult time."

Sela placed her hands on both hips and frowned. "Save your hollow platitudes, Bolrakei. The clans may have restored you to your former position, but I haven't forgotten your treachery against the dragon riders. Your betrayal of one of our own has not been forgiven."

The fake smile dropped from Bolrakei's face. "What are you doing here then? I certainly don't remember inviting you."

Sela looked like she wanted to strike her. Skemtun would have applauded her for it. Instead, Sela said, "The dragon riders are here because it is our job to protect the people of Durn. I've come to deliver this." She reached into her waistband and produced a scroll, which she handed to the spellcaster standing near the front of the carriage. "I would've gotten this message to you sooner, but the only dwarf telepath is Mugla, and she left Mount Velik to serve the Vardmiters. There was no way to deliver this message to you any faster."

The old dwarf wizard reached into a breast pocket. He took out an ancient pair of spectacles and placed them carefully on his nose. Then he slowly unrolled the parchment. Skemtun glanced at it, but the parchment was blank.

Mumbling to himself, the old wizard said, "There's a minor glamour here ...*Pārēre,*" he said, waving his fingers over the scroll. The glamour dropped, and hidden runes appeared. The old man squinted, struggling to read the tiny writing.

Bolrakei's brow furrowed. She tapped her foot impatiently. Finally she said, "Speak up! What's taking you so long? What does the message say?"

The old mage shook violently. His eyes were wide, his hands trembling. Lifting his weathered face, he whispered, "I can't believe it... this can't be happening now. Not now!"

"What? What is it? Don't just stand there! Tell us!" Bolrakei screamed. When the old man failed to respond, she reached out and slapped his hand, knocking the scroll into the dirt. "Say something, you doddering old fool!"

The wizard's voice came out as a choked whisper. "The orcs are on the march. They are coming here, to Mount Velik. They mean to overrun our city."

A chorus of frightened cries rose from the crowd.

Sela raised her hands and spoke. "Calm yourselves, please. It's true. The greenskins intercepted one of your funeral announcements. King Nar gathered his armies the very same day. The orcs are coming here, and they will arrive at your doorstep before the next full moon. I'm sorry, but the funeral ceremony must end now. In a few weeks, the greenskins will be at your doors, and Mount Velik will be under siege."

"It's too soon!" Bolrakei shrieked, "We just started rebuilding after those blasted Vardmiters left! Our troops aren't ready for combat—we're not prepared for it!"

Skemtun looked at the Sela, and then at the frightened crowd behind him. It was a sea of terrified faces.

It was true, then. The orcs were coming. Skemtun didn't want to believe it, but he couldn't deny it. "We'll have to get ready," he said softly, "because we don't know when they'll strike. We don't have any choice." He raised his voice and spoke to the crowd. "Everybody turn around. We have to go back inside... and get ready. The clans must prepare for battle."

Sela nodded. "War is coming, whether you like it or not."

Part 2: The Orc Menace

Tallin's Fight

Tallin woke up in a dark place. He turned over and groaned. His wrists and ankles were tied with rope, and his head felt like it was on fire. Tallin strained against the ropes and cursed. The knots only grew tighter.

The elves had enchanted the bonds. He should have known it wouldn't be so easy. A1 He struggled to sit up, gasping as pain shot through his limbs. Every muscle in his body ached and it was all he could do to remain upright.

He blinked into the darkness. As his eyes adjusted, his surroundings slowly came into focus. He was inside a small room with a wooden floor. There was no furniture, just a few light crystals embedded into the walls. The crystals gave off a dim red light that distorted the color of everything. He checked for a door, but there was none, just a narrow opening on the far side of the room.

He reached up and touched his face, and found clotted blood near his ear. *How long have I been here?* He glanced around, tried to find other options, but the room was empty. There was nothing he could use to break his bonds. There was no way he could escape.

"Hello?" he called into the darkness. "Is anyone there?"

He heard a grunt and the sound of light footsteps. Carnesîr and Fëanor walked into the room.

"Well, look who's finally awake," Fëanor said, gesturing toward Tallin. "You've had a good sleep, *half-ling,* snoring like a contented hog for days and days. I thought you were never going to wake up. A single hit and you went down like a bag of sand. You mortals are such fragile creatures."

"Untie me, you bastards," Tallin said, kicking his bound feet up and down. The skin on his wrists and ankles stung as the rope dug into the flesh. The more he struggled, the more the ropes tightened.

A strange light flickered in Carnesîr's eyes. "Please don't aggravate him, Fëanor. We need the dwarf to be cooperative."

They were talking about him like he wasn't even there. Tallin wanted to scream and throw a thousand curses their way, but he forced himself to remain calm. Angering them wasn't going to do him any good. "Cooperative?" Tallin asked. "What makes you think I'm going to cooperate with you?"

Smiling sweetly, Carnesîr said, "Don't force our hand. I would prefer to avoid using... *questionable* interrogation methods."

Tallin glared at him and strained against his bonds. He flinched when the ropes tightened again.

"Don't bother trying to escape," Carnesîr said. "The ropes are enchanted, and I cast the spell myself. Trust me. You aren't going anywhere until I release you." He walked in a slow circle around Tallin, checking the ropes carefully.

Tallin looked around the room. His mind was clearing now; things were becoming real again. "Where am I? Where have you taken me?"

"We're still in the same forest," Carnesîr said, "about a league away from the Elder Willow. Fëanor is quite adept at nature spells, so he constructed a proper shelter for you. Wasn't that nice of him? This is a hollowed-out tree that wasn't hollow a few days ago. It took a fair amount of energy to create. You should be thankful."

Backwards elf logic, Tallin thought. *I should be thankful that they didn't kill me.* Tallin leaned back against the wall. "So what do you want?"

"Just a little information. Tell us what we need to know, and we won't have any problems."

Tallin kept silent, and Carnesîr stalked angrily to his side. "Look, we know that you overheard us. You know very well what we're talking about. Don't play stupid with us."

"I'm not talking. I don't care what you do to me," Tallin said.

Carnesîr's voice became low and honey-sweet. "I would hate to cause you needless pain. Come now... tell us where the dragon's nest is. We checked on it a day ago and now it's gone. Where did the female move her nest? Tell us... we only want to help you."

"You can forget it. I'm not telling you anything," Tallin repeated.

Carnesîr's smile became darker, but he continued. "We only want to help. We want to protect the eggs. That's all! Think about the future of dragonkind. Why don't you just cooperate with us? Tell us where they are. Be reasonable."

Tallin stared straight ahead, as if he hadn't heard him. A loud buzzing filled his ears and kept getting louder as the seconds ticked by. He winced. His protective wards had been activated. Luckily, he always kept his warding spells refreshed. But that wouldn't work forever—eventually the strain would be too much, and he would pass out again. Trying to fight the elves' manipulative spells was draining, painful even, when they were physically close.

Carnesîr tried again, this time with a scolding voice, like a schoolteacher talking to a naughty child. "Don't make this difficult! We don't want to force the information out of you. Mortal minds are weak—we can force you to tell us anything we want to know. Truly, I would prefer if you would just tell me."

"Oh, don't worry about that," Tallin said, grimacing. "Once I tell the other dragon riders about this, *they'll* be the ones making things difficult for *you*."

The buzzing in Tallin's ears amplified. He tried to ignore it, but his head felt like it was going to split in two.

Fëanor sighed. "This is ridiculous! Please remind me why we're negotiating with this dwarf?" He jabbed his finger at Tallin. "Just tell us where the eggs are! We'll force you to tell us!"

Tallin glanced at Fëanor, a mocking smile tugging at his lips. "You can certainly try, you insufferable, arrogant bastard. You can certainly try. But don't hold your breath. I'm quite good at resisting elf magic."

Carnesîr's smile dropped. "We are very determined." He spit the words out like cannon fire.

"I'm sure you are," Tallin said.

"Well, have it your way then. The hard way." Carnesîr reached out and placed his hand on Tallin's shoulder. Tallin closed his eyes and prepared for the inevitable. He knew this wouldn't be pleasant, but how far would they really go? As Tallin felt Carnesîr's magic begin to surge, a scream erupted from outside. The elves spun around.

"That's Amandila's voice!" Fëanor shouted, and they both fled outside. Tallin wiggled his body toward the entrance and peered outside.

Duskeye was there, belching fire and smoke as he rampaged through the forest. He swung his enormous head from side to side, smelling the air. *"I know Tallin is here! Give me back my rider!"* he bellowed.

There were multiple fires burning behind him. Duskeye opened his jaws, scorching the trees with a stream of fire. Branches burst into flame, sending up plumes of black smoke.

Amandila hid behind a giant elm, peeking out from the back with terrified, rabbit-like eyes. Duskeye sent a column of fire in the elf's direction.

"Help me!" she cried out to the others. Tallin watched as she ducked back behind the tree. She wasn't using any magic to defend herself. He figured she was torn between wanting to defend herself and not wanting to injure one of the few remaining dragons.

Fëanor moved forward to help her, but he was too late. Duskeye roared, shooting a spiraling gout of flame in her direction. She had the wits to summon a shield in time to block the fire, but she wasn't fast enough to avoid Duskeye's swinging tail.

Duskeye hit the elf so hard that she vaulted through the air, hit a tree trunk, and crumpled to the ground. She balled up into a circle and moaned. The dragon moved forward, his muscled legs gliding over the tree roots.

Duskeye blinked his good eye and snarled, *"I can sense Tallin's presence. My dragon stone tells me that he's here! Where is my rider? Tell me now, or I'll fry you both to a crisp."*

"Let me take care of this," Fëanor said, stepping forward. He raised a glowing palm. "Be calm, *dragon-friend*. We don't wish to hurt you." Coils of light danced on the elf's fingertips. His voice was cloying, seductive and enticing. The air filled with a sickly-sweet perfume.

Duskeye hesitated and moved back, his nostrils twitching. Fëanor smiled, whispering softly while the fire raged around them. "Yes, yes, I am your friend, and you shall *obey* me."

Duskeye swayed back and forth, and his eyes glazed over.

Fëanor moved closer and closer, coaxing and nodding. When the elf was within a few steps of him, Duskeye sprang on Fëanor. The elf screamed and his hands flew up to his face. Duskeye grabbed the elf by the neck and squeezed, flexing the elf's hollow bones under his grip. Fëanor's eyes bulged, and he clawed desperately at the dragon's paw.

"You fools! Did you really think I could be deceived so easily? Your pathetic faerie spells have no effect on me. I am warded against your trickery!"

Fëanor squirmed in his grip, then gasped and went limp. Duskeye jerked the elf into the air and flung his body as far as he could. Fëanor hit a tree with a loud thump and fell to the ground.

The furious dragon spun around to face Carnesîr. Duskeye reared up on his hind legs and advanced, his face a mask of rage. *"You're the only one left, elf. Would you like the same treatment as your friends?"*

Carnesîr jerked backwards, his hands raised. "Now, now... let's be civilized, shall we? There's no need for violence."

"Where is Tallin? Tell me now! I'll carve you up without a second thought, elf, believe me!"

"I am not your enemy, Duskeye!" he replied, his lips twitching. He kept stepping back, but Duskeye matched his pace.

The dragon stared him down. *"For the last time, where is my rider? Release him now or I'll burn this entire forest to the ground. You might escape, but those two unconscious friends of yours won't make it. Immortal or no, nothing can survive being charred to a crisp."* The dragon's voice sounded like crushed gravel.

"Binvigi!" Carnesîr shouted. A pulse of searing energy shot from his hand and hit Duskeye's thigh. The dragon howled, his leg buckling underneath him. Duskeye let loose another stream of flame. Carnesîr summoned a shield and blocked it.

From behind, Tallin cried out, "Duskeye! I'm over here!"

The dragon pulled himself back up and turned again on Carnesîr. *"Release him now, or by the gods, you will feel my wrath."*

Carnesîr squirmed under Duskeye's hard glare. The elf chewed his bottom lip and looked anxiously at his friends.

Amandila and Fëanor were both unconscious. Fëanor's arm was bent at an unnatural angle. Even from a distance, Carnesîr could see it was broken. The elf's shoulders sagged. "All right!" he finally relented, raising his hands in surrender. "I'll release the dwarf." He flicked an index finger in Tallin's direction. *"Halda-Lauss."*

The enchanted ropes fell away and Tallin stood to his feet, rubbing his tender wrists. "Thank you, friend." He went over and embraced Duskeye tightly. "I was hoping you would find me. The elves kept me unconscious, and they cast a spell to prevent me from contacting you."

"I know. I've been searching this area for days. I could sense your general location, but I couldn't pinpoint it. As soon as you awakened, I knew exactly where you were. The dragon stone called out to me like a beacon. Elves can't control everything." He leaned forward, carefully inspecting his rider. *"Did they hurt you?"*

"No, no. They sure threatened me, but they didn't harm me," Tallin said. "I'm a dragon rider, after all. They wouldn't have killed me. The elves aren't that contemptible."

Just then, he felt dizzy. Tallin staggered on his feet as the world began to spin. He leaned against Duskeye's side and closed his eyes. His skin itched and his face felt unbearably hot.

"What's wrong?" the dragon asked.

"Elf magic," whispered Tallin. "It's wearing off," He grit his teeth, fighting waves of nausea as the elvish spells died. His carefully crafted wards never faltered, but blocking elf magic always had physical repercussions. He gulped air until the wooziness passed. Then he turned to Carnesîr, who was standing nearby. The silver-haired elf didn't look the least bit sorry. In fact, he seemed to take pleasure in Tallin's discomfort.

"Why did you do this?" Tallin asked. "What do the elves want with this dragon's nest?"

Carnesîr sniffed. "I'm not at liberty to say. Our queen ordered us to retrieve the dragon eggs and take them back to Brighthollow with us."

"But you're a dragon rider, too! For *Baghra's sake!* Why would you do something so cruel to the female? You know that dragons can go insane if they lose their nest. Shesha has suffered enough already!"

Carnesîr's face colored a bit. "Look, I have my orders. The queen told us that the nest is in danger and that she wanted to save the eggs. That's all."

A short distance away, Amandila groaned and sat up. She ran her fingers over her ribs and grimaced. Seconds later, Fëanor woke up, his breath coming in shrill gasps. "My arm!" he cried. "My arm is broken!"

Amandila crawled over to Fëanor and placed a glowing hand on his chest. She shot Duskeye a look. "His arm is shattered, and so are two of my ribs!"

"You'll live," Duskeye grunted. *"Don't expect me to feel sorry for you after what you've done. You shouldn't have tried to hurt my rider. Maybe next time you'll think twice before you do something so stupid."*

Amandila scowled but didn't respond. She stayed by Fëanor's side, healing his injuries with magic.

145

"You roughed them up quite a bit," Tallin said quietly.

Duskeye shrugged. *"I wasn't trying to kill them, otherwise they would be in far worse shape. Besides, they aren't my concern. Wolves don't concern themselves with the opinions of sheep."*

Tallin gave a short bark of laughter. He knew the elves would never apologize, but neither would he. "I see your point." Tallin turned around and spoke telepathically to Duskeye. *"Where is Shesha? Are the eggs safe?"*

"Yes," replied Duskeye. *"As soon as I received your message, I moved them. Now they're near the desert border. I warned Shesha to be vigilant and not to leave the nest unattended. If she senses any more danger, I told her to fly to Parthos with the eggs. She wasn't happy about that, but she promised she would do it. She trusts us, at least."*

"Good," Tallin said.

By then, Amandila and Fëanor had limped over to where they were standing. Fëanor had healed most of his injuries, but he still had to lean against Amandila in order to walk.

Carnesîr had regained his composure and was now smiling. "Now that we've stopped all this pettiness, I do hope we can have a civilized conversation."

Tallin felt like raging at the elves for what they had done. Instead, he let out a deep breath and answered calmly, "How can you possibly expect me to forget this took place? You, Carnesîr, of all people, should know me better. You took me hostage. You held me against my will. You separated me from Duskeye. And now you want to sit and chat like we're old chums?"

Carnesîr paused for a moment before replying. "We did what we thought was necessary. It's—it's a very complicated issue."

"I'm sure it seems that way to you. You'd better tell me what this is all about, or I'll send a message to the dragon riders that I was kidnapped by the elves. That won't bode well for you, I promise."

Carnesîr scowled.

"Don't tell this *halfling* anything!" Amandila said, her cheeks bulging. "Xiiltharra has forbidden it!"

"Oh, Amandila, relax, he already knows about our plans. He overheard our conversation in the forest. What's the harm in him knowing the rest?" Carnesîr shrugged. "The time for deception is over."

She eyed Tallin contemptuously. "Humph! Meddlesome dwarf!"

Carnesîr ran his hands over his face. "Here's the truth. Fëanor has been patrolling the western coastline for months. He intercepted a message originating from Balbor Island. Their priests know about the nest. They already know the nest's basic location. Their assassins are excellent trackers. The Balborites want to capture all the eggs and the breeding female. The priests have already sent several men to search for it. I caught one of them myself less than a fortnight ago. He was a sly one, but I managed to kill him in the end. They're bound to send more."

Tallin looked confused. "But why would the priests want dragon eggs? There are no dragons on Balbor Island. There never have been."

The elves exchanged furtive glances. Carnesîr scratched his cheek and looked away, avoiding Tallin's eyes. "Ah... well... that's not entirely true."

"What?" Tallin asked. "What do you mean?"

"Thousands of years ago, the Balborites had their own dragon riders. They trained and bred them on the island. Balborite breeders are the reason why there are black dragons today. Their breeders selectively bred for that color over hundreds of years. Eventually, they began destroying all the eggs that wouldn't produce black dragons. They wanted a uniform species. As time passed, the Balborite religion became even more bloodthirsty and bizarre. The priests started to look for ways to strengthen their power. They used stolen elf magic to cross their black dragons with another animal. That's how the *drask* lizards were created. The priests even went so far as to sell breeding pairs of this loathsome new creature to the orcs. The elves considered this an abomination. At that point, our queen intervened."

He reeled back for a moment. "They created *drask?* So what happened next?"

Carnesîr looked down and shuffled his feet.

Fëanor snorted. "Go on, then! Why are you stopping now? You've gone this far. You might as well tell the dwarf everything."

Carnesîr continued, "A group of elf warriors stormed the island. All the Balborite dragons were slaughtered, and their drask, too. Unfortunately, we couldn't eradicate the drask from the mainland. The orcs had already bred several thousand of the creatures and it was too late for that."

"If all the black dragons were killed, why do we have black dragons on the mainland? We have two in Parthos right now."

"The queen thought it would be cruel to destroy the eggs, so any black eggs that were discovered were taken back to the mainland and fostered there. This was a long time ago, and there were plenty of female dragons willing to foster an egg. The Balborites were warned that if they ever attempted to breed dragons again, the same thing would happen. They haven't attempted anything for centuries, but time has passed, and mortals have very short memories. It doesn't surprise me that they would try something again after a few thousand years."

Tallin couldn't believe what he was hearing, but the more he thought about it, the more it made sense. The Balborites were capable of all kinds of atrocities. Why not this? "So the Balborites want their own dragon riders. That's insane." He shook his head.

"Yes, we realize that. Which is why we're here. It's crazy, but the priests are certain to follow through with this ridiculous plan, regardless of the consequences or the negligible chance of success."

"How long has Brighthollow known about this plot?" asked Tallin.

"We discovered it only recently. Less than a moon ago. Our queen sent us to recover the eggs before the Balborites could get to them."

Tallin frowned. "Why didn't your people notify Parthos? We could have worked together on this. Despite everything that's happened, Parthos and Brighthollow are allies. We're not your enemies."

Carnesîr sighed. "Our queen deemed the information too sensitive to share. She feared that if she announced the plot, the Balborites might destroy all the eggs before we had the chance to recover them. When the first message was intercepted, she was unsure whether the Balborites had already sent their assassins to the mainland. So she kept the information a secret."

Tallin looked up. "That's not the only reason she kept quiet. She also knew the dragon riders would go to war over this."

"Ah... perhaps." Carnesîr smoothed the front of his tunic, trying not to meet Tallin's gaze.

"Listen," Tallin said, "this problem isn't going away. Stealing the eggs from the nest isn't going to solve anything. We have to do something about the Balborites."

Now Fëanor spoke up. "The elves already know this. We've dealt with these insufferable fools on some level or another for thousands of years. Once they've got an idea in their heads, you can forget about changing their minds, no matter how illogical, irrational, or dangerous it is. They're difficult to frighten, and they're willing to die for their cause, however misguided it may be. Any opposition actually reinforces their commitment to whatever ridiculous plan they've hatched. Now that their high priest has issued this order, the Balborites would rather destroy the entire nest than have the eggs fall into anyone else's hands. There's no middle ground with them."

There was a moment of silence. Tallin's head was still buzzing from before, and now with this new information, it felt like a hornet's nest. He tried to clear his senses. "Perhaps we're approaching the problem from the wrong angle."

"What do you mean?" Carnesîr asked. "Our plan is good. We care about the safety of the nest. The eggs would be safe at Brighthollow, where no mortals may follow." Then he paused. "But... if you have a better idea, I'm willing to listen."

Tallin cleared his throat. "Why wait for them to attack us? Why not go on the offensive? We could go to Balbor in secret, like the elves did before. A small raiding party could reach the island quickly. Have any of you ever been to the island?"

Carnesîr and Amandila shook their heads, but Fëanor spoke up. "I've been there. Many years ago, before I was linked to my dragon. Balbor is a dreary place, much different from the other mortal lands. The whole island is rocky, and most of the land is inaccessible on horseback. The roads are terrible. The towns are small and spread apart. They only have one major city, and that's where the main temple is located. There are lots of priests and assassins, but only a few freeborn commoners. Social status is very important there—the most important thing after religion is the class one belongs to. The freeborns wear yellow shirts to distinguish themselves from the rest of the populace. No one else is allowed to wear that color."

Tallin looked confused. "So there aren't many people in the city?"

Fëanor shook his head. "No, there are plenty of *people*, but most of them are slaves, with a smaller number of indentured servants. Slaves are badly treated by the higher classes. Priests are the highest social class. They kill slaves without a second thought, as easily as one would kill an insect."

"How many mageborns are there? Do you know?"

Fëanor shrugged. "It's impossible to say. All their assassins are mageborn. It's a requirement. But I don't know if they train all the mageborns that they find. They have seeker-priests that go out into the countryside and search for them. I assume that they must find mageborns among the slave populace quite often. How could they not? There are countless slaves on the island, but I only counted a handful of freemen in the city. On Balbor, thousands of slaves are exploited by a small number of masters."

Tallin scratched his beard, brooding over what they should do. "What is Balbor's greatest weakness?"

"Their religion," said Fëanor. "They're extremists. And extremists don't behave like normal individuals. Religious fanatics don't think things through or make wise decisions. The temple is the center of their society, literally and figuratively. That's where one should strike in order to cause unrest."

Tallin pursed his lips. "What about the high priest himself? Is he vulnerable to attack?"

Fëanor shook his head. "No, he's under constant guard. He wouldn't be an easy target, or even a valuable one. Killing the high priest would cause only a temporary disruption. The Balborites have a complex order of succession, and there are plenty of others waiting in line to replace him."

"What would happen if the temple was destroyed?" Tallin asked.

"That would cause serious turmoil. It would be a catastrophe for them. It's the center of their daily life. But to destroy the temple would be impossible."

"Nothing is impossible," Tallin said. "Describe the building. What does it look like? How big is it?"

"It's a vast structure in the center of their capital. Much bigger than any cathedral on the mainland. The interior is constructed of cut stone, and the roof is ceramic tile. There's the main building, which is larger than any fortress on the mainland. The structure has a main library, and few smaller libraries that are private. There's an infirmary, and a huge training center for the acolytes. Nothing is made of wood, so it wouldn't be as simple as burning it down."

"Is the temple heavily guarded?"

Fëanor thought about it. "Not as heavily guarded as one might expect. The exterior guards are servants, not trained soldiers. They are there mainly to deter theft. There are a few soldiers inside the main chamber, but not many. Since outsiders aren't allowed on the island, an attack on the temple itself would be unthinkable. It's almost impossible to get onto the island because Balbor has so many protection wards placed on it. Anything larger than a sailboat will activate the wards. They simply wouldn't expect any type of major attack."

"Did you see any assassins while you were on the island?"

Fëanor nodded. "Yes, several. Most were in various stages of their training and only had partial tattoos on their bodies. I only observed them from afar. It was easy to avoid them; they're proud of their warding tattoos and wear minimal clothing to display them. I didn't want to risk revealing my true identity, so I didn't interact with them at all. I just stayed out of their way."

Tallin asked, "How do you know so much about this?" The question had been simmering at the back of his brain ever since Fëanor started talking.

The elf shrugged. "I was curious about mortals in my youth. I traveled all over the continent, including Balbor. It was easy enough to get on the island. When I reached the city, I posed as a slave. A simple glamour

155

was enough to walk freely among them, although I did take a beating once. In order to protect my disguise, I didn't fight back, which was infuriating. I left shortly after that. That's it. I didn't discover anything terribly interesting. I played a few tricks on them, of course, but the Balborites are poor targets for practical jokes. Zealotry breeds stupidity, and playing with fools gets tiresome quickly. The Balborites are, for the most part, stupid and cruel. They weren't as interesting as I'd hoped they'd be."

The four of them stood in silence for a moment. Then Tallin said, "The dragon eggs are in danger. As long as the Balborite priests want them, they won't be safe. We have to attack the source of the danger."

"But why risk it? We have an easy solution," Carnesîr pleaded. "Let us take them! The eggs will be safe in Brighthollow!"

"And what happens when there's another nest? Will you steal those eggs, too? No. I won't allow that. Shesha, the dragon female, knows of your plans. Duskeye relayed the information to her, and she's gone to a safe place. Shesha will fight to the death before she allows anyone to take her eggs."

Becoming angry, Duskeye stepped forward, warning the elf, *"I'll say this just once. Those eggs are my offspring. Don't try anymore tricks on us, and leave the nest alone—or I'll kill you."*

Carnesîr's face reddened. *"Humph!* You don't have to be so rude about it. We were only trying to help."

Tallin dusted off his trousers and mounted Duskeye's back. He looked at the elves. "As I see it, you've got two choices. You can all go back crying to your queen empty-handed, or you can accompany me to Balbor and try to stop the problem at its source. The other dragon riders are busy elsewhere. No one else can help me do this, and I'm going for sure. So are you coming with me or not?"

Carnesîr stared wordlessly at Tallin for a moment. Finally, he sighed. "I guess we're going to Balbor."

The Oath of Enemies

T allin and Duskeye flew back to the Elder Willow. When they touched down onto the ground, Mugla scurried forward, grabbing her nephew in a rough embrace.

"Ye've been gone for days!" she said. "Where were ye? I was worried sick! Why didn't ye respond to my telepathic calls?"

"I'm sorry," Tallin said. "I ran into a bit of trouble with the elves." He told her everything that had happened, including his kidnapping, and about his plan to attack the Balborite temple.

"Oh no!" Mugla said, placing her hand over her mouth. "Ye can't go to Balbor!"

"I have to, there's no other way. I have to do something about the Balborites, before they destroy the nest. The elves have agreed to help me. They're coming along."

"Well, that's better, I guess. But still... ye need extra help. I'm comin' with ye." She nodded as if she was the one giving approval.

"No way. That's absolutely out of the question," Tallin declared.

"But I insist. I'm coming with ye," she repeated. "I've thought it over very carefully."

"It's impossible that you've thought it over very carefully... because I just told you a few minutes ago." He took a deep breath. He admired her fiery resolve but he was starting to lose patience. "Please don't fight me on this. It's too dangerous for you."

"Too dangerous for me, but not too dangerous for you? You're barely a child!"

"I'm a grown man."

She poked her finger at his chest. "Fah! Fah! A little hair on your chin doesn't make you a man, so don't be smart with me. Besides, I'm a lot more powerful than ye give me credit for. I saved yer life just a few weeks ago, didn't I? Or have you forgotten that already?"

Tallin sighed. She was his aunt, after all, and no matter how much she exasperated him, he had to show some respect. "No. I haven't forgotten. You did save me... and I'm very grateful for that. But this is different. We aren't fighting a single assassin. Balbor is crawling with them."

"So I'm supposed to stay here and twiddle my thumbs? Or go back to the dwarf caverns while ye sail over to Balbor and risk yer skin?"

"Well, you did say that you had a responsibility to the Vardmiters," Tallin countered, his determination wavering. He didn't sound very convincing, even to himself.

"I've got a responsibility to ye too. Ye're my nephew, and I promised yer mother I would take care of ye. Believe me, ye could use my help! I've visited Balbor before, and I'm familiar with the lay of the land."

He stared at her. *"You've* been to Balbor? When was this? Did you go by yourself?"

"Yes, of course I went all by myself," she replied, laughter in her voice. "It was about two hundred years ago, when I was a lot younger. That's when I was still crafting weapons, mind ye. I had an enchanted sword and several fantastic daggers on me. Magnificent stuff, really."

He raised one eyebrow. "I'll admit you've piqued my interest. Why did you go?"

"To take back my bloody spell book! They stole it from me. The Balborites aren't just assassins—they're also notorious thieves. When their priests find out the location of a valuable spell book, they send out their minions to steal it. Long ago, one of their temple assassins snuck into Mount Velik and stole my grandmother's grimoire. The book had been handed down for generations—it was priceless. I went to Balbor to steal it back."

The story seemed inconceivable. But he knew his aunt wasn't lying. "Were you able to find the book?"

"Yes, I did get it back, though it wasn't easy. First, I took a little sailboat to the island. I landed at night, on the northern shore, where their wards are weaker. From there, I walked to the main city where the temple libraries are located. It took a long time to walk, many days of travel, but I took my time. When I got to the main city, I searched the library for days before I found it."

"Were you discovered?"

Mugla shrugged. "No. I dressed shabbily and pretended I was cleanin' the shelves. That allowed me to look at all the books. Eventually, I found it, but I didn't just take it and leave. I swapped out the real grimoire for a fake! I wanted to teach 'em a lesson. I put a bunch of false spells in there. I'm sure it took a while for them to realize that the book they had wasn't real. My little trick singed off more than a few eyebrows, I'm sure!" she cackled. "Two can play at their little game!"

"How did you travel unnoticed?"

"Oh, I posed as a servant. No one suspected me. Some ratty clothing coupled with a bit of humility will make anyone invisible. I just kept my head down. I've

161

been spellcasting for hundreds of years and I've learned how to hide myself quite well. A single individual can pass through their defenses. Ye just have to stay away from all the mageborns, they can sense other spellcasters."

A corner of Tallin's mouth lifted. "You surprise me. It seems I've underestimated you once again, dear aunt. I will not do so again."

Mugla reached up and patted his cheek, her mouth stretched in a toothless grin. "Apology accepted, my dear. Well, if we're going to do this, we'd best be going. We have several days of hard travel ahead. Let's say goodbye to Chua and Starclaw. When we get to the coast, we'll need to commission a sailboat. It's not possible to fly into Balbor on a dragon. The perimeter of the island is warded. To pass through the wards unnoticed, ye must travel on foot."

Tallin blew out his cheeks. "That puts a wrinkle in our plans. I wonder why the elves didn't tell me that important detail."

Mugla shrugged. "It's possible that they didn't know. Or simply forgot. Or didn't care enough to tell ye. Or the wards might not affect them. A hundred reasons spring to mind. Elves only seem to retain information that directly interests them. They don't worry about the Balborites, for the most part. I think the elves view them as rather silly and not very dangerous."

"But the Balborites *are* dangerous. They've been a threat to us for years."

"A threat to *mortals*, yes, but to the elves? The Balborites are not a threat to them. The magic of the elvish lands is too powerful, none of the mortal races can travel there, and that includes the Balborites, even their powerful Blood Masters. Believe me; the elves have only a passing interest in this, perhaps because they're bored, or because the Balborites are threatening the dragons directly. That's the only reason why they've agreed to help ye."

Tallin leaned back against a tree, his mind tossing and turning. "You're probably right. It's understandable why Carnesîr and his little band of elf lackeys would be interested in this mission. But who knows for sure what their motives are? Queen Xiiltharra may finally want to intercede and save the dragons. She's never been overly concerned before. But now, with this new nest she may have changed her mind, even if her methods are misguided."

"Just don't expect too much from them," she said. "Elves only concern themselves with mortals when they're protecting their own interests. Knowing them as I do, they'll never do anything unless pushed."

Tallin nodded. "There's some external pressure at work here, and I'm not sure what it is yet, but I'm determined to find out. But first, we have to stop the Balborites. If they get their hands on those dragon eggs, we'll be in far worse shape than if the elves had taken them. The elves wouldn't try to harm the eggs, at least not intentionally. I can't say the same for the Balborites."

"That's for sure. Now, when are we going?" Mugla asked, folding her hands in her lap.

Tallin sighed. "I planned to leave today. The elves are traveling through the countryside on foot, and I don't have a rendezvous point yet. I've got to contact Carnesîr using a mind spell."

Mugla grimaced. "Ugh! I don't envy you there. Contacting elves that way is the worst. They're manipulative telepaths."

He wasn't looking forward to it, either. Tallin already disliked using telepathic communication. It was exhausting and always felt like an invasion of privacy, but contacting an elf this way was a whole different level of discomfort. He hated to do it, but there was no other option.

"Well, I may as well get this over with. I'll be back." He needed to find a quiet place where he could concentrate.

"Ye'll do fine. Stay strong. Don't let them sift through your memories—they always like to do that." Mugla stood up and wrapped her arms around him.

Tallin nodded and padded into the forest. He hated doing this. Anything would be better than linking his mind with an elf's.

He stopped at a large oak tree that grew near the path. It was as good a place as any. Tallin sat down, closed his eyes, and leaned his head back. The old language came out effortlessly as he opened his mind to the spell. His consciousness drifted out, touching the edges of other minds. Ribbons of blue light surrounded his body. He sensed Carnesîr's mind pushing against his like a coiled spring.

Glistening with sweat and breathing hard, Tallin felt the elf's mind wrap around his like a snake. Tallin struggled to fight the assault, putting up blocks to protect his memories, but the elf's telepathic powers were greater than his. He could sense that the elf was laughing at him, enjoying his humiliation.

Carnesîr sifted through Tallin's memories and thoughts, stripping his mind bare. Carnesîr was a vindictive telepath, and with Tallin, the elf was settling a score. Every moment was like a knife in Tallin's brain. He clenched his teeth against the pain.

Tallin had allowed the initial contact, so his wards couldn't help him. He had to endure the elf's invasion of his privacy. Carnesîr finished his exploration of Tallin's private thoughts, and quickly relayed the information regarding their location and the rendezvous point. Then Carnesîr withdrew his mind sharply, stabbing backwards with a mind shield as he exited.

Tallin dropped to the ground in a heap, and his world went dark. He awoke several hours later with his heart pounding a steady drumbeat in his ears. The conversation came back to him then, all of it roaring back into his head like a dam-break.

He took a deep breath and let his lungs fill up slowly. He struggled to get up, leaned over, and vomited. He still felt incredibly dizzy. He steadied himself with difficulty, reeling like a drunken man, careful not to make any sudden moves. He shuffled miserably back to the grove, where his aunt Mugla was waiting for him.

Mugla was peeling fruit on the grass, holding a bowl in her lap. When Tallin came closer, she jumped up and grasped his shoulder. "Are ye all right? Ye look as pale as a ghost! Were ye able to get the information ye needed, at least?"

Tallin nodded and groaned. Even that tiny movement made his head pound. "Yes, I contacted Carnesîr, then he attacked me with a mind shield. What a surprise."

"I'm sorry, dear. Ye look a bit green. Here, eat this. It's star fruit with a dash of numbweed. It will ease your headache. The numbweed doesn't taste very good, but the star fruit does. "She pushed the bowl in his direction. "The elves are terrible that way. So what did he say?"

"The elves are meeting us on the coast, on the western edge of the Elburgian Mountains. They'll be able to run for days without tiring, but even so, it will take them a long time to reach the coastline on foot. If they're lucky, they'll find some horses, but I wouldn't bet on it. "

"Did ye ask the elves about their dragons? Did Poth, Blacktooth, and Nagendra agree to help, or are the elves' dragons going to remain in Brighthollow and let the elves fend for themselves?"

"Carnesîr refused to talk about it. It's a touchy subject for him, apparently."

"Humph." Mugla crossed her arms. "Something's going on. It's unusual for a dragon rider to go on a mission alone, and that goes double for an elf-rider. There's more to this story than meets the eye. Ye can bet on it."

"I'm sure you're right. I have that feeling, too. Come on, let's go talk to Chua. We should be on our way soon." Before leaving, they stopped to say goodbye to Chua and Starclaw, who they found sitting underneath the Elder Willow.

"Goodbye, Chua," Mugla said, reaching over to embrace the fragile mage. "We just got here a few days ago, and now we're leaving again. I'll come back for a visit as soon as I can. I still owe ye a bowl of yams."

Chua laughed. "I'll hold you to that. I want a bigger bowl next time!"

Mugla reached over to squeeze Starclaw's massive green leg. "I'll miss ye too, Starclaw. Take care of him for me, will ye?"

"*Always,*" Starclaw said with a razor-sharp smile. A wisp of smoke escaped her snout.

"Wait, before you go, let me give you something." Chua grabbed a handful of earth and sprinkled it into her palm, muttering a short spell. The soil turned into a silver powder. "Save this sparkling earth. If you're attacked, throw it in your attacker's eyes. They'll fall asleep instantly."

Mugla removed a leather pouch from her pocket and funneled the glimmering powder into it. "Thank ye," she said. She strung the pouch on a piece of string and put it around her neck. "I appreciate it, but I hope we won't need this."

"Me either, but it's there if you need it. Take care of yourself, Mugla. And you too, Tallin. Good luck on your journey."

Chua smiled. He waved them off, saying, "I won't hold you up any longer. You should go now, before it gets too dark. Goodbye." His voice sounded clipped.

Tallin felt a pang of foreboding as they spoke. Chua seemed anxious. Tallin tried to ignore the feeling, chalking it up to nerves. Chua had the Sight, and if he didn't say anything, what could be wrong?

Starclaw and Duskeye said their goodbyes too—quietly and respectfully as dragons do.

Duskeye pumped his powerful wings and took flight, lurching into the air with Tallin and Mugla on his back. Wind whistled around them. Mugla shouted a final farewell as they left the forest floor. "Goodbye, you old soothsayer!" She was smiling and waving even though she knew that Chua couldn't see her. Tallin and Mugla disappeared above the trees and soon they were gone.

Chua let his hand fall to his side and took a deep breath. The sound of the dragon's wings died away in the distance. "Thank goodness they've left."

Starclaw crawled forward to sit next to Chua. She rested her giant emerald head on his lap. *"How do you feel?"* she asked.

Chua sighed. "I feel tired. Weak." Then he shrugged. "I'm relieved that Tallin and Mugla left when they did. That's all that matters."

He felt peaceful, yet sad. A contradiction of life. It was quiet for a moment. Two white butterflies fluttered through the clearing. The breeze settled around him, fresh and fragrant.

"The grove is really quiet this evening," Chua said suddenly.

"You always knew this day would come," Starclaw said.

"Yes, I always knew," he replied. "I've always felt the burden in my heart."

"Are you frightened?" she whispered.

Chua shook his head. "Not really." Then he gave her a soft smile. "Well, maybe... but just a little."

The old rider and his dragon sat in silence until the sun sank over the mountains behind them. The night cooled, and the smell of the evening flowers swirled around them. Buzzing mosquitoes surrounded Chua like a cloud, and he muttered a quick removal spell to shoo them away.

Chua shivered and drew his blanket around his shoulders. Darkness fell, and small creatures emerged from their burrows, scampering through the long grass as they searched for their evening meals.

The mischievous tree sprites played in the branches above him; they were always the most active at twilight. There were hundreds of them in the trees now. The moon rose slowly in the sky, casting its pale white light onto the grove. Suddenly, a wave of silence settled over the forest. The sprites ceased their chatter, the birds stopped chirping, and even the wind stopped moving through the trees.

Chua froze. *It was happening.* He raised his face and sniffed the air. The breeze carried a foul odor, dark and putrid.

"She's here," he whispered, *"and she's casting a black spell."*

A loud hissing, followed by thousands of tiny cries, pierced the silence. An instant later, he felt them falling around him. The tree sprites fell by the hundreds, shrieking their pitiful death rattles, their little bodies crumpling into heaps around him. They fell on his shoulders, in his lap, and on the soft grass around him. For once, Chua was thankful that he couldn't see.

"What's happening?" asked Starclaw, shaking her head.

Chua drew a sharp breath. "She's killing all the tree sprites. She knew about them, about how they're charged with defending this sacred place. They would have attacked her, so she killed them before they could."

"The Elder Willow is unprotected then," Starclaw said in a hushed voice.

"Yes. Darkness has fallen over this place." Chua waited, remembering his visions. He knew what would happen now. He felt powerless to stop it.

Skera-Kina stepped out from her hiding place in the trees. A thin trickle of blood dripped from her nose. She wiped the blood away with the back of her hand, leaving a crimson streak across her cheek. Her chest heaved and her body shook, but she looked triumphant.

Her face was flushed, but she looked around with clear eyes. The tree sprites, wild creatures of the forest, lay scattered within the sacred grove that they had protected for centuries, their broken limbs and tangled hair leaving a grisly pattern on the grass. Skera-Kina looked down at the tiny green bodies. She threw back her head and roared with victory. Chua knew that the spell had cost her much, but it had worked. The tree sprites were all dead.

Taking a deep breath, Skera-Kina opened her eyes and instinctively knew that there was nothing for her to fear. She smirked, raising a tattooed finger into the air, as if to test the wind. Her sharpened teeth gleamed in the moonlight. "There you are," she whispered.

Chua gulped air to ease the tightness in his chest. *If only I was younger and not a cripple...* but no, those days were gone. It was no use trying to imagine it. Chua did not attempt to flee or hide himself. He had seen this coming and had known the outcome for years. There was no escape.

Skera-Kina stepped forward, her black leather boots moving silently through the grass. She stopped a few paces away from the old spellcaster. "So, you're the great oracle of the east." She studied his face, and saw the resignation written there.

"I am he," Chua responded flatly, "if you wish to call me that, I suppose."

"You don't look like much. I didn't expect a cripple." Her deep voice sounded like two stones grinding together.

"Appearances can be deceiving, dark lady."

"Indeed," Skera-Kina said. "Indeed, they can be."

Chua threw off his blanket and propped himself up as best he could, facing his adversary. Starclaw tucked her shattered wing behind her and wrapped her tail around her rider.

Chua cleared his throat. "Say your piece, then."

Skera-Kina cocked her head to one side. "You know that I'm more powerful than you. Even if you were in perfect health and not the broken creature that you are, I would still have twice your strength. You cannot hope to defeat me in the state you're in, old man."

Chua seemed to deflate suddenly. "I know this. I have foreseen it."

Her eyebrows rose. "That's not the response I expected. You're much calmer about this situation than I thought you would be. Are you not afraid?"

Chua removed his blindfold. He stared in her direction with eyeless sockets. "I am not afraid of you. Look at me. Look at my broken body and my scarred face. I know what real pain is. There is nothing left for me to fear in this life. Any real fear died within me long ago." Starclaw was stoic and quiet, but her sorrow was palpable. She was blind and crippled, too. She wasn't strong enough to defend her rider, or prevent their fate.

"You have a stout heart," Skera-Kina said, her voice carrying a small measure of respect. "Most fear me."

"I'm sure that's true. But my soul is at peace with this. My duty was to live my life in a way that was pleasing to the gods and to be ready to depart whenever they wished it." He raised his chin. "Do what you must."

She stood back for a moment, observing Chua carefully. "I propose a bargain, then. You can certainly choose to fight me. But you shall lose, and your death shall be unpleasant, as will the death of your dragon. Instead, I propose a pact between us, an agreement that will benefit us equally."

"Go on."

"You are an oracle. Tell me my future, honestly and truthfully, and I'll grant you an easy death, without any suffering. It's a fair trade." Her voice held no rancor.

Chua considered the request. "I'll only answer questions about you. Not about anyone else. And you must give Starclaw an easy death too, if she desires it."

After a moment, she nodded. "Agreed."

"I accept this pact. I am an oracle, and it seems fitting that this will be my final reading."

"Swear to it, then. In the old language."

Chua spat into his palm. *"Sannindi,"* he said. The air around him sparked. "Now you must swear in turn." It was the *Oath of Enemies.* Now they were sworn to tell the truth. The spell could not be broken while either party was still alive. Chua wheezed, gasping for breath. The effort of such a powerful spell had taken the energy out of him.

He felt weak... weaker than he had in years.

Skera-Kina spat into her palm. *"Sannindi,"* she said. The air sparked again. Chua reached out to touch Starclaw and was comforted when he felt her cool scales under his hand. When his breathing returned to normal, he said, "I can't walk. You must come and sit by me."

Skera-Kina slid through the grass like a snake and made her way to where Chua lay against the massive truck of the ancient tree. The sounds of the forest were slowly returning, and now crickets could be heard in the grass.

"Please sit here," Chua said, spreading out his hand. He invited Skera-Kina to take a seat on the grass. "The foretelling will be more accurate if I can touch you."

Skera-Kina paused, and then crossed her legs and sank down into the grass. Her shoulders remained arched and alert, ready to strike at a moment's notice. She kept one hand on the hilt of her dagger, and stretched the other one out to touch Chua's arm. He flinched at the contact, but did not pull away.

He inhaled, and his face took on a faraway look. "I'm ready to answer your questions. What is it that you want to know?"

Skera-Kina pondered for a moment, and then spoke. "I was born a slave, and throughout my life, I've had many masters. I have always lived a life of submission. First to my slave master, and then to the great Temple of Balbor."

She paused. When she continued, her voice was subdued. "I am a Blood Master and the highest ranking spellcaster in all of Balbor. My position is one of great honor, but... in my soul, I wish for freedom. I have taken a blood oath to the temple. Sometimes, I wish that I had not." She raised her face. Behind the swirling tattoos, her eyes danced with a haunted glow. "I am tired, old man. I have been forced into a life of perpetual servitude. Will I ever be free?"

He took a deep breath. "You wanted the truth, and you shall have it. You were not born a slave, as you believe. You were born free in the caverns of Mount Velik. And you are not human. You are a dwarfling, born to a dwarf mother and an elf father. That is why you are drawn to the dwarves. They are your people."

Skera-Kina was so startled that she jerked her hand away. "I'm not human? I'm half-elf? Am I immortal, then?"

"No, only *pure-blood* elves are immortal, and you are a *half-blood*. However, your life shall be very long, assuming you don't die by violence. Unless you can break your blood-oath, you shall be forced to serve the temple for hundreds of years. The priests must have known you were mixed blood when they forced you to make your dedication. They knew you would potentially serve them for a long, long time."

"If I was born free, then how did I become a slave?"

"Because of the war. Slavery wasn't outlawed until after the war was over. Do you know Druknor Theoric?"

Chua's words raised the hair on the back of her neck. "Yes... he's the constable of Sut-Burr."

"That's the one. You must know him; since he is one of your spies."

Skera-Kina nodded. The oath would have prevented her from lying anyway, so she admitted it. "Yes, he is. Druknor is a Balborite spy. He has been reporting intelligence to our priests for decades."

"You were sold into slavery when you were a baby; by him—Druknor Theoric. He is the one responsible for your current condition. You would never have been sold into slavery if it were not for him. He kidnapped you from your adopted family and sold you to the Balborites."

Skera-Kina clenched her fists until her knuckles went white. "That snake.... I should have slit his throat when I had the chance."

"...But you did not," Chua said.

"No. I've been tempted to kill him so many times. But Druknor is useful to the temple priests."

"He's not as useful as they've been led to believe," Chua said. "He's a double agent, and he's been feeding misinformation to your priests for a long time. Druknor cares nothing for your religion or your cause. He's only interested in stuffing his coffers with gold and securing more power for himself in the north. He's never stopped smuggling; all of those profits he keeps for himself. The dragon riders recently discovered the depth and breadth of his crimes, so Druknor's days are numbered. When they finally get the evidence to convict him, he'll face execution."

Skera-Kina shot him a glance. "If what you say is true, and he is a traitor to Balbor, then I'll gut him myself. I've stayed my hand one too many times with him already. Arrgh!" Skera-Kina paused for a moment to control her anger. "Will I ever be relieved from this bondage?"

"Unfortunately that answer is not clear to me. Your blood oath binds you to the high priest, and your pledge to the temple is irrevocable. You chose to take the blood oath of your own free will. You must adhere to it, and you can't simply walk away from the obligation. As long as the high priest lives, you are compelled to follow his orders. You cannot harm him yourself, either directly or indirectly. Your oath prevents that."

"So I am trapped in this life," she said with a hollow laugh.

"Your blood oath binds you forever, but you still have *some* choices," Chua said. "They are choices with vast implications, but they are yours to make. You can escape the oath by taking your own life. You can also wait for the high priest to die."

"That doesn't sound like much of a choice," she replied.

Chua shrugged. "It's still a choice. There are some oaths that reach beyond death, and you are lucky that yours does not extend to the afterlife. And the choice is closer than you think. Soon, the gods shall grant you a single opportunity to decide your fate. At that time, you shall decide whether to continue your life as it is, or break free."

"When?" she asked. "When will this be? Tell me exactly."

"My foresight is not exact. But it will be soon. Within a year, perhaps."

After a while she stood up and brushed the pine needles off her tunic. There was nothing more to say. "Thank you for the information. Are we finished here?"

"Yes," said Chua, the words barely escaping his lips.

"Prepare yourself then." She drew her sword from the sheath on her back.

Chua sighed. He had the gift of Sight—he always knew this day was coming. He had known it for years, but now tears flowed down his scarred cheeks.

"One moment please." He reached over and caressed Starclaw's massive jaw. The dragon purred into his hand, nuzzling her rider with her snout. "Thank you for being my dearest companion for all these years," he said quietly. "After everything we have suffered together, I thought I would never shed another tear, but now, so close to the end, I feel that my heart will burst inside my chest."

Sorrow bubbled up inside him. But there was something else too—a feeling of freedom, a kind of liberation that he would finally be free from this life—free from this tortured existence.

Starclaw's tail tightened around her rider. *"Thank you for being with me through every storm."*

His face softened. "I love you, my dearest friend," he said, his voice choked with emotion. Chua wiped his nose and lifted his chin, keeping his hands at his sides. He did not attempt to defend himself. This was his time to die with dignity.

"This death is a gift, old man. Don't move or flinch, and I promise you won't feel any pain. My aim is true."

Chua nodded. "I am ready then."

The sword hissed through the air as she swung it, plunging it deep into Chua's heart. She kept her promise—her aim was true. He gasped once and fell forward.

With one quick pull, she withdrew the sword from Chua's chest. Without wiping the blade, she did the same to Starclaw. The dragon didn't flinch, but she cried out Chua's name in dragon-tongue before she died. After a few kicks, Starclaw lay still.

Skera-Kina leaned over their bodies and tore the dragon stones from their chests. She held the two halves in her cupped palms. They were beautiful, sparkling like emeralds in the moonlight. But the beauty only lasted an instant.

As Chua and Starclaw died, the stones slowly turned cloudy and gray, and then splintered into a handful of shattered shards. The once-beautiful stones now looked like common rubble. Skera-Kina opened her hands, and the fragments tumbled onto the grass.

Skera-Kina raised a glowing hand and cried out, "*Incêndio!*" The fire twirled and spun, sucking up air into its inferno. Her dark eyes watched the fire flicker and grow. The flames surged up toward the Elder Willow.

A burning limb broke off and fell to the ground near her feet. The willow became completely engulfed. The fire spread, and soon the entire grove was ablaze, hot sparks flying everywhere.

The fire licked toward Chua's lifeless body and the flames consumed the body of the spellcaster. As his flesh burned, a black bird with a brilliant red crest landed in a tree nearby. It screeched, calling out to its mistress.

"Come to me!" Skera-Kina ordered, reaching out her arm. The huge raven flew from its perch and landed on her shoulder.

"*The eyes! The eyes!*" it cawed.

Skera-Kina shook her head. "Sorry, my dearest. Not this time. I couldn't save the eyes for you. This poor wretch didn't have any!" She laughed, and the bird seemed to laugh, too.

Pleased with her handiwork, the assassin turned and left.

Preparing for War

King Hergung's funeral procession was promptly canceled, and all the mourners filed back inside Mount Velik. Sela and Elias, the two visiting dragon riders from Parthos, followed the line of mourners through the iron gates and back into the caverns. Their dragons, Nydeired and Brinsop, stayed outside the mountain, taking to the sky to patrol the area.

Twelve dwarf guardsmen were posted outside the gates, and more were added the following day.

As soon as word spread that the orcs were coming, all the visitors started packing. Everyone knew that the orcs would have no qualms about slaughtering them all, even in the midst of their king's funeral. A group of dwarves, all draped in heavy cloaks, took Hergung's body off the ornate litter and carried it back up to his former chambers.

The council decided to bury Hergung without fanfare the following morning. All the visiting dignitaries were politely asked to leave—not that they needed any convincing. They left in fear, scrambling to put as much distance as possible between themselves and the orc horde.

The atmosphere inside the city changed. There was no time to waste. The orc armies marched toward them, and now everyone had to prepare for the imminent siege. Word spread throughout the mountain. Rumors grew. The clans were upset. After all the turmoil they had suffered the last few years, why should they have to go through this now?

Sela and Elias requested a meeting of the dwarf council, and the high families were summoned. This time, no one argued.

Now that King Hergung was dead, the highest ranking clan leader, Bolrakei, sat at the head of the table. Her face was drawn and had deep lines from lack of sleep. Skemtun sat to her right, with his ever-present bodyguard, Kathir, standing behind his chair. Bolrakei's advisors gathered behind her.

The chairs on Bolrakei's immediate left were for guests, the two dragon riders. Sela and Elias stepped forward and sat down. The remainder of the council, highborn dwarves from influential families, took their seats. The room was packed. One dwarf tapped the table, keeping an inconsistent beat. Another fidgeted with his garments. Everyone was nervous, and no one knew what to say.

Skemtun leaned back and crossed his fingers over his belly. He motioned and said, "Mistress Sela, please speak."

Sela stood up and cleared her throat. "Thank you, Councilmember. Thank you for allowing me to address the council today and provide an update on the situation with the orcs. This is what we know for sure; the greenskins are on the march. They're traveling on foot, but they also have mounted cavalry on drask. The horde is enormous—much larger than I anticipated. The fate of your race now rests in the balance."

"How many orcs are there?" asked Skemtun.

"Their numbers have swelled in recent years. In fact, I've never seen an orc horde this large. There are many thousands, but we don't have an accurate count yet." An alarmed murmur rose around the table.

One of the other councilmembers raised his hand. His face was young, with just a hint of whiskers poking through his chin. "Excuse me? What is a drask? Is that some sort of animal?"

Sela turned her head slightly, as if thinking about what to say. "Drask are a cross between a dragon and a common lizard. The orcs train them like horses and value them very highly. A drask's bite is deadly; their saliva is so toxic that the orcs tip their arrows with it. The orcs are a mortal race, and they have no mageborns among them, so no one knows for sure how the orcs were able to create and breed such a ghastly creature to begin with."

Bolrakei shivered. She was afraid of orcs, but even more afraid of their *drask*. "How—how many drask are there?" she asked, her voice wavering.

"A least a thousand; but probably more. When we passed over the horde, I saw them moving in a solid block at the front."

Bolrakei gulped. The orcs brought their drask to Mount Velik during the last Orc War, and Bolrakei remembered seeing the fearful lizards pounce on a dwarf soldier, covering him with bites. Even though the bite wounds were shallow, the soldier died an agonizing death. The toxin in the lizard's bite was so poisonous that even the best healers weren't able to save him. The poor man's screams of pain had haunted her for years afterwards.

Skemtun said, "Since the elves hate the orcs so much, why haven't they offered to help us? Don't they know that the orcs are coming here to destroy us?"

Sela's mouth twisted. "The elf queen is aware of what's happening—that much is certain. But you cannot depend on the elves. They help us only when they feel like it, and there's no reason to believe they'll come to your rescue. Your clans are on their own."

"What made the orcs decide to attack us now? Why, now, of all times? Why now?" an older woman with jet black hair asked, her hands tearing through her hair.

"If I was your enemy," she said slowly but firmly, "I would certainly attack you now. Your clans are fragmented and your king is dead. The orcs knew about the funeral, as well as your civil war with the Vardmiters. You never made any attempt to keep it quiet. Your kingdom's vulnerabilities were broadcast for everyone to know."

The dark-haired woman started sobbing. "We should have kept Hergung's death a secret. We should have drawn together, instead of making such a big fuss!"

Bolrakei gave the woman a hard look. "Be quiet, Amara. Stop your blubbering. It's embarrassing." Then she turned to Sela with a hopeful look. "What if the orcs decide to attack the Vardmiters first? That would give us extra time to prepare."

"Given the military weakness of the Vardmiters, such an attack would be successful, but it's unlikely," Sela said. "The Highport Mountains are not an attractive target for the greenskins. Highport is a tangled maze of massive, unfinished caves. It's too cold. It's likely that Nar scouted the location before the Vardmiters occupied it and decided that it was unsuitable for his needs."

"Are you sure?" asked Bolrakei, a hint of desperation in her voice.

"Yes. The orcs are moving steadily through the Trautt Plains in this direction. They've never shown any interest in the Highport caves. They want *this* mountain."

"We were just beginning to recover from the ordeal with the Vardmiters," said Bolrakei. "We aren't in any shape to fight the orcs."

The dwarves slouched in their chairs. They looked defeated.

Elias finally spoke. As a healer, he was dressed entirely in white robes, and his face was shaved clean. "You have no choice but to fight," he said quietly. "I've watched the horde's movement. The countryside is in ruins. The orcs are destroying everything in their path. They are monsters. You cannot negotiate with them. If you wish to survive, then you must fight."

Bolrakei wrung her hands. "But how can we possibly defend ourselves against such huge numbers? You say there are thousands of them. Thousands! How can we defeat them, especially with our own numbers so low? We don't have enough men!"

"You must remain calm. You've beaten them before." Sela's expression was stern, a rock in the sea of desperate faces. "The last Orc War wasn't so long ago. Many of you remember it."

A grizzled old dwarf snorted from the corner of the room. He had a tiny claw hammer hanging from a chain around his neck. "Sure! I remember it! Last time the orcs attacked, we barely survived! We had an army, a healthy king, an' the help of the elves. How can we hope to fight against 'em now?"

More frightened muttering rippled through the group.

Sela waited until the dwarves quieted down before she continued. "Look, I suggest that you stop worrying and begin doing something useful. Every able-bodied man should be given a sword and sent to military practice. You have plenty of weapons in your armory, so that's a mark in your favor. Your soldiers can make camp outside the mountain and begin training in earnest tomorrow morning. Your spellcasters should prepare healing potions. Elias is very skilled at this, so he will help you. The women should begin stockpiling food. It's likely that there will be a long siege. Everyone must work together."

"How much time do we have to prepare?" Bolrakei asked quietly. Her expression was oddly calm, as if the truth of their situation was finally sinking in.

"A few weeks. Perhaps a month, but not more than that," Sela said. "Orcs run fast and sleep little. They destroy the countryside as they move, so they never stay in one place for more than a single day. I was able to warn the villagers in time to evacuate, but most people didn't have time to grab anything other than a few belongings. There's a sea of devastation behind horde, as there always is. They'll just keep moving— they won't stop until they get here. Based on their current progress, the greenskins will be here by the next full moon."

Sela withdrew a scroll from a fold in her cloak and unrolled it on the tabletop. It was an intricate map of the surrounding area. She pointed at the top of the map. "Each square you see is fifty leagues. A drask can cover forty leagues in a single day. Once they cross the Orvasse, the drask will be here within two days, assuming they move ahead of the rest. The infantry will take another week to arrive."

Skemtun pointed at the map. "They have to cross the river. Why don't we destroy the bridge near Ironport? Will that stop them?"

"No. Destroying bridges has never stopped them before. Orcs are skilled raft builders. They'll strip the surrounding forest and create huge rafts to carry their army across the river. Destroying the bridge will delay them for only a few days, and it will make it harder for any support troops to cross."

"Spread the word," Skemtun ordered. "Notify all the clans. We must set aside funds and supplies. Preparations shall begin tonight."

Everyone on the council nodded their agreement.

Skemtun stepped out of the meeting in time to watch messengers race out to all the highborn families. Their news was simple: prepare for war. This time, there were no complaints, no objections. The dwarves rushed to work.

King Hergung's body was laid to rest the following morning. Mourners formed a line to view the body, scuttling past, throwing flowers or muttering a quick prayer. The eulogies were hurried and somewhat insincere.

Although tears were shed, there was no feast after the ceremony. After that, siege preparations began in earnest. All the incense pots were snuffed out, and oil-saving torches were placed along the corridors.

Soldiers dragged vats of oil up to the walls above the gate. Women collected firewood and built the fires that would keep the oil boiling hot. They stocked the lookout tower with provisions and manned it with guards.

Water was not a concern, at least. A deep spring flowed through the mountain, supplying the dwarves with all the water they needed. But food stores were limited, as they had been for years. Women went out into the surrounding forest, searching outside the mountain for tubers, acorns; anything that was edible and could be stored. Food that had been prepared for the king's funeral was set aside and preserved. The magnificent funeral oxen were slaughtered, but instead of preparing the meat for a feast, the beef was sliced into strips, dried, and stored.

While the men trained to fight, the women worked to prepare everything else. They gathered food, cut firewood, and tended the goatherds. Children made bandages and worked in small groups to organize the supplies. They ran errands and helped any way they could.

Soldiers prepared trenches around the gates, and the men started training. Years of peace had made the dwarf troops complacent and lazy, but that changed quickly when the clans nominated a grizzled old captain named Baltas to take over the soldiers' training.

Baltas was old—older than Skemtun and Bolrakei put together. He was missing an ear and two fingers on his right hand. He walked with a pronounced limp that came from an axe wound suffered during battle. But even with his old age and injuries, he was the toughest fighter in the kingdom.

Skemtun went outside on the first day to see how things were going. Baltas walked around the makeshift camp, inspecting the men. Hundreds of young soldiers stood at attention. Baltas took one look at the bedraggled troops and grinned, rubbing his hands together with glee.

"There's not much time to whip these lads into shape," he said, his eyes twinkling with mischief. "But ah'm sure going t' try!"

Being charged with guarding Mount Velik from the orcs was a big responsibility, and Baltas took his job very seriously. Each day, he marched his tired, sweaty troops up the mountain and then down again. He forced them to practice drills until they were ready to collapse.

The older dwarves weren't spared; they were pushed just as hard as the young ones. Those with fighting experience were put in charge of smaller groups. All of them trained from sunup to sundown.

Inside the mountain, Elias worked closely with the dwarf spellcasters to craft and stockpile healing potions. Sela and her dragon patrolled the forest and the surrounding areas. The days turned into weeks, and all the while the dwarves continued their feverish preparations.

At the end of the month, there were several days of fog, followed by heavy rain. The ground outside the mountain turned into a muddy soup and the training camps were full of misery. But still, the training continued unabated, week after week.

When the skies cleared and the sun broke through, the orcs came into view. Clearly visible from afar, the armies looked like an immense green serpent slithering toward Mount Velik.

At the back of the horde were supply carts filled with livestock, likely stolen from the small villages that were scattered across the plains. As Sela had predicted, mounted drask led the infantry. She sounded the alarm and sent word to all the clans that Mount Velik would be under attack within days.

The training camp was dismantled, and the dwarf soldiers withdrew inside the mountain. Watchmen took up their posts on the ramparts. Women and children moved into deeper caves for safety.

Ironically, these were the same caves that the Vardmiters occupied before they left.

There was only one main gate outside the mountain, but there were several secret entrances that were much smaller. Soldiers were stationed at the smaller entrances, too, in order to make sure no orcs snuck inside. The main gate was reinforced with warding spells. Heavy iron bars were welded on the inside. Goats and other livestock were collected into pens inside the mountain.

The dragon riders now alternated patrols, scouting the horde's progress day and night. The unbearable stench from thousands of unwashed bodies wafted through the air and made flying downwind from the horde almost unbearable. Orcs did not bathe, and their muscled green bodies were smeared with rancid animal fat.

Flying on their dragons, Sela and Elias watched the orcs march down into the shallow valley outside Mount Velik. The enemy trudged steadily forward.

Skemtun stood outside and looked out into the distance. He drew a deep, tired breath. He was scared, for himself and for his people.

Were they ready? Were they strong enough to survive the impending battle? Had they the strength to endure to the end?

The Horde

Baltas' nostrils flared. He marched down the line of trembling soldiers, barking orders, admonishing the men to look sharp. He was in charge of all the troops now, including the archers.

The dwarf council had pushed for someone younger, but Baltas had more experience than anyone else. He would lead their soldiers well in this fight, if they could overcome their fear.

"Keep your chin up, lads!" Baltas cried encouragingly. The men did their best to comply. "We're here to fight, fight, fight!"

Skemtun followed the grizzled drill instructor as he made his rounds, checking the troops for fitness. Most of the soldiers looked so young, and their fighting skills weren't very good. Training had started as soon as they found out that the orcs were coming, but the dwarves had precious little time to prepare. All the troops needed work.

Skemtun had fought against the orcs when he was younger, back when his beard was still dark and his hands weren't knotted with age. He still vividly remembered the fighting; the feeling of triumph when they finally won. The whole experience seemed so long ago, but it felt good to step inside that place again and remember.

The troops spent long days practicing swordplay and other skills. Skemtun offered support where he could. Sometimes he threw himself into the drills, hurling practice blows, jumping over ropes, and fighting with wooden weapons. In reality, he wasn't much of a fighter, but he did his best to keep up, and he never complained. He wanted the troops to see him, to know that he was running the gauntlet as they were. He tried to inspire the younger men, to spur them along. The younger ones were the most eager to learn.

Skemtun was still a clan leader, after all. All the troops tried to impress him, even those from other clans. When Skemtun was around, they grunted louder and ran faster, showing off their newly-acquired combat skills. He encouraged them to do more for themselves.

We don't have much time to prepare, and the odds are stacked against us... but at least my presence seems to boost their morale.

After those training days, Skemtun dragged his aching body home and soaked his limbs in the hottest water he could tolerate. The following morning, he could barely move. But he managed it, and always came back to the training camp the next day. It all felt good in a way, despite the pain. It helped distract him from the terrible reality they were facing.

They needed more. More supplies. More catapults. More arrows. More vats of boiling oil. More of everything.

All sorts of necessary equipment were in short supply. Worst of all, they didn't have enough soldiers. They were especially short on trained archers. The archers were their first line of defense. What good are a thousand bows if you don't have archers to shoot them?

Kathir had been right about everything. Their kingdom was unprepared for war. It showed in their meager supplies, their frightened troops. And now it was too late to do anything about it, too late to train more soldiers.

All the dwarves wore solid plate armor with chain mail underneath. At least they had that. The armor was heavy, cumbersome, but it was worth it. *Good armor saves lives.*

Skemtun thought about Kathir and recalled their conversation on that fateful day, weeks ago. It was so difficult to think about.

Kathir had popped into his life and brought with him an avalanche of bad news. How very long ago it seemed. He remembered their exchange verbatim, he remembered his own denial of the looming crisis and the impending war, how he'd disregarded those fateful warnings. Unfortunately, everything Kathir predicted had come true. Their king had died, and the orcs had begun their war march, but it wasn't until Sela arrived in a panic that they knew the orcs were coming.

"I should 'a listened to Kathir," Skemtun muttered to himself. "We would've had more time to prepare. My stupid pride got the best o' me, and we've lost precious days because o' my stubbornness. Now time is on our heels."

To his credit, Kathir never brought up the subject again. He didn't try to make Skemtun feel guilty about ignoring his warnings. Kathir simply took up his position as bodyguard and followed Skemtun around the mountain. With an understanding that he would be notified as soon as the assault began, Kathir went into the dwarf caverns to help the others gather some final provisions.

Kathir had been right about the Vardmiters as well. Mount Velik needed their numbers, if only as support for the troops. But worst of all, the Vardmiters were now safe from the orcs—the orcs weren't going to attack Highport Mountain.

The Highport caves simply did not interest the orcs. And who could blame them? The Highport caverns were a terrible place to live—poorly designed, dark, damp, and so cold that ice often formed inside the caves at night.

Just weeks ago, he had asked himself why anyone would want to live there. Now he knew differently. The Vardmiters were secure in their new stronghold, while his clan would be fighting for their lives at Mount Velik. Once again, it seemed that the Vardmiters would have the last laugh.

Our entire kingdom is in jeopardy. They should be here, helping us fight!

"If only," he had pondered countless times, "if only the Vardmiters hadn't left when they did, we'd have more men, more supplies..." How many times had he agonized over the same thing in the last few days? Try as he might, he couldn't stop the thoughts from echoing in his mind. The constant anxiety chipped away at his confidence.

He stopped and stared blankly into the distance. It just wasn't fair.

Baltas turned and barked at him. "Why are ye starin' off into space? Are ye daydreamin'?"

Baltas was still trooping up and down the line shouting orders, and Skemtun realized he had slipped away into his thoughts... again. Skemtun breathed in sharply, trying to clear his head. "Sorry, I drifted off there for a bit."

"Well, pay attention and stay alert. Are ye comin' along, or not?" Baltas demanded after a pause.

"I'm comin', I'm comin'," Skemtun huffed, jogging forward to catch up with Baltas.

"Hurry up, now. We've got a lot o' work to do today. It's time to pack up the gear and get ready." Two short blasts on a war horn signaled that it was time to break camp. Everyone scrambled to transport everything inside.

The dragon riders had given them an early warning. The first wave of orc troops was less than a day's march away. Skemtun squinted. He could just make out quivering trees in the distance. Somewhere in the forest, a tree fell with a crash, sending frightened birds flying up around it. They were out there, somewhere, moving and hiding in the trees. The beating of war drums was now clearly audible; a constant hammering that shook the dwarves' resolve.

Black dust rose up around them as they marched forward. The orcs trudged over the land with hunched backs, their weapons dragging behind them. They didn't march in a straight line like dwarves or men, but in jumbled clusters.

The horde gathered just outside the tree line and waited there. What he saw in the distance was a mere fraction of what lay in the trees. They teemed at the forest's edge like a giant ball of maggots. Skemtun shook his head and groaned. The dragon riders had warned them that the orcs' numbers were deceiving. Behind the horde, a great swath of forest burned with greasy black smoke.

Within a short while, the orcs would be standing before their gates, surrounding Mount Velik with their foul presence. The orcs were out there, moving towards them. They were out for blood. The orcs wouldn't stop until Mount Velik was captured.

It's either us... or them.

The two dragon riders, Sela Matu and Elias Dorgumir, patrolled the skies. They observed the horde as it traveled across the plains, burning everything in its path. Both dragon riders had been reporting information to the dwarves for several weeks. The news wasn't good, and it seemed to get worse every day. Trying to estimate the orcs' numbers was nearly impossible. The first count was ten thousand enemy troops. That seemed implausible at the time, but still manageable. Then, the number rose to fifteen thousand. Last night, Sela told them there could be as many as twenty thousand orc troops. That didn't even include the drask.

Sela and her red dragon Brinsop patrolled the west. Elias and his white dragon Nydeired patrolled the forests outside Mount Velik. Just yesterday, Nydeired had found and killed an orc scout.

While the orcs' numbers swelled, the number of dwarf troops remained the same. Their small contingent of soldiers, barely three thousand men, would have to be enough. There simply weren't any more men. All the women, children, and the elderly were moved into a deep cavern in the mountain, which had a secret passageway outside... if it came to that.

Skemtun sighed and tried to concentrate on the task at hand. Along the walls, young soldiers tended to fires that blazed under vats of boiling oil. The soldiers stirred the oil and kept it hot.

Two dwarf spellcasters set protective wards behind the lines. There were four remaining dwarf spellcasters, and they had been ordered into the caverns below to protect the women and children. If the mountain was breached, those spellcasters would use protection spells to get the rest of the people to safety.

Skemtun hoped that wouldn't be necessary. He stopped to shake hands with a friend, speaking briefly to the man. A throng pressed around him good-naturedly, each man wanting to shake hands or share stories.

The ranks of soldiers stiffened to attention as Baltas trotted along the wall, doing his final check of their defenses.

Then Baltas stopped in front of a young dwarf who was crouching down, his hands on his knees.

Grabbing his chain mail, Baltas wrenched him upright. Baltas' forehead wrinkled unhappily as he looked into the young dwarf's terrified eyes. "What's wrong, whelp? Are ye goin' to be sick?"

The dwarf was young, barely twenty seasons old. His pallor was ashen, and his eyes were red-rimmed from crying. "No, sir. Nothin' wrong at all." He sniffed and wiped his nose with the back of his hand.

"Don't look like nothin' to me. Why're ye blubberin'? Be strong my boy!"

The soldier hiccupped and didn't respond. The words of encouragement didn't seem to help.

Skemtun stepped toward him and placed his hands on the young dwarf's shoulders. "Look, laddie, it's all right to be scared. Sometimes I'm scared too. But no matter what happens, remember Mount Velik needs ye." The young man sniffed and nodded, but he looked even more miserable than before.

Skemtun glanced down at the ground and slowly shook his head. "Wait, forget that. Forget about Mount Velik."

Baltas leaned forward, his tiny pebble eyes scrunched up. "Eh? What are ye playin' at?" he demanded in a furious whisper. "Have ye lost yer marbles?"

Skemtun silenced Baltas with a wave of the hand. "Tell me, son, which clan are ye from?"

"I'm from *Klorra-Kanna*, sir," the boy explained in a halting voice. "I... I volunteered to fight."

Skemtun tried not to make a rude face. *Ugh, Klorra-Kanna...Bolrakei's clan. But he's just a boy, and he's afraid like all the others. Maybe clan loyalties don't matter so much, especially at a time like this.*

Skemtun held up his hand. "Just give me a minute. Look, forget yer clan, too. Don't fight for them. I don't care what ye've been told by other folks. None o' that matters now."

"Then...then what are we fighting for?" asked the young soldier.

Skemtun's voice rose. He spoke loud enough for the crowd around him to hear. "Do not fight for our kingdom, or even for yer clan." He paused. Every head was turned, their eyes trained on him. "Nay! Fight for yer mother! For yer father! Fight for the ones ye love and for what ye believe in! Never give up!" he shouted.

A circle of bright-eyed dwarves surrounded him.

Skemtun hopped on top of a crate so everyone could see him. He stood tall and raised his arms. "I'm speakin' to ye today, not as a clan leader, but as a brother and friend! We're all part of the same family!"

206

Scattered cheers rose from the crowd. They were starting to feel it. He was giving them a shred of hope. Skemtun gave them a beaming smile. He was never much of an orator, but now the words spilled out of him like water from a pitcher.

"Aye, the greenskins are a menace! To everyone! But don't be afraid! This is our chance to prove our worth! I believe in ye! We'll leave this fight victorious! Don't forget the faces of yer brothers and sisters, mothers and fathers. And don't forget the brothers standin' right beside ye, either. And most of all, don't forget your courage! It's there, deep inside of ye, just waitin' to come out!" His words rang loud and clear through the air.

There were more cries from the troops. "We'll follow ye, Skemtun!"

Skemtun drew his battle axe from his belt and raised it in the air. All the soldiers followed his example. "Use yer heart! Let it guide yer axe. Fight now, without fear—to live another day with yer loved ones!" Skemtun's speech struck a chord. Other soldiers took note of his words and joined the cheering crowd. "Death may stalk us, but it won't defeat us. Not today! Not tomorrow! Not ever!"

The troops responded with a deafening cheer. *"Yea, Skemtun! Yea, Skemtun!"* they hollered with one voice, fists pumping in the air. Their cries rose like thunder, drowning out the sound of the orcs' war drums.

Skemtun stepped down from the crate and walked back to where Baltas was standing. His head was held high, and the bright sun shone across his brow. Baltas came up and clapped him on the shoulder. A rough smile had transformed the captain's rugged features. "A mighty fine speech, old friend. Mighty fine, indeed. Ye sure riled 'em up!"

Skemtun chuckled. "Aye, I hoped it would, I truly did. The words just came out and, well, it worked, didn't it?" The soldiers were all smiling now, whooping and jumping, shouting war cries. Some even started yelling battle songs. "They're all set then?"

Baltas glanced up and down the line. "Seems so. They look ready to fight now. When the orcs reach the front gate, it starts. To be honest, I wish it'd happen sooner rather than later. The waitin' is the worst part, ye know? For me, anyway. For these poor lads, it's murder."

Skemtun stopped at a gap in the stone battlements. Carvers had been working day and night to reinforce the walls above the gates and had doubled them in size. The wall they stood on ran above the main gate, looping back into the mountain. The gate, made of heavy iron, rested beneath them, cemented deep into the thick stone walls.

Behind them was a narrow entrance to the mountain and the dwarf city beyond. Skemtun glanced down at the walkway, which could accommodate twelve dwarves walking abreast. It was made of thick stone. Good stone. And heavily warded too. Dwarf spellcasters reinforced the wards again this morning at dawn. These walls were strong.

The dwarves had built these defenses eons ago. Beneath a rocky outcropping above the main gate, stonecutters had collected the thickest stones they could find and began to build. They built the wall up tall, leaving only a small gap between it and the top of the mountain. The battle tower was carved right into the mountainside, making it impossible to scale.

"How's everything inside the city?" he asked.

Baltas shrugged. "As good as can be expected, I guess. The women and children are scared out of their minds, but there's not much we can do about that." Skemtun ran his free hand over the smooth rock and sighed. Yes, they would defend the gates. They would hold strong. They had to.

Could we have built the walls up a little more? A little higher? Would it be enough?

Looking at the horde in the distance, Skemtun had his doubts. He feared for the outcome of the battle. There were just so many orcs—too many of them. He began to hear their shrieks in the fields below.

They were so close.

The afternoon passed in a distressing haze. Skemtun refused to leave the walls, deciding to stay on watch through the night. He stood behind the ramparts, playing nervously with his axe.

When evening fell, a small contingent of greenskins made their first approach, and were soon standing before the gate. The orcs started hammering on the doors with their weapons, making as much noise as possible. They lifted their spears in a display of force, the bone handles reflecting the moonlight.

Another squadron marched into the orchard and raised their torches into the branches. The dwarves' precious fruit trees went up in flames. The air became heavy with the scent of burning leaves and trampled grass. All of the trees would be charred and black by the next morning. The orcs barked and bellowed, pleased with their first act of destruction.

The orcs had bows resting on their backs, and the feathered tips of arrows stuck up behind their tusked heads. Some wore grisly-looking armor, constructed from bones, which were then sewn onto animal skin. Others wore plain leather armor, and the rest wore nothing but loincloths. They were abominably filthy and emitted a smell so foul that some dwarves were sickened by it. Skemtun stepped back from the parapet. "Are we going to try and push 'em back?"

Baltas shook his head and held up his hand, ordering the dwarves to wait. "Not yet. If we fire too soon, our arrows will be wasted. If we were fightin' a normal army, our first volley might scare some of them off. But this isn't a normal army. The greenskins will never break and run. Best to wait a while."

The dwarves maintained their positions and waited. The minutes ticked by, and the orcs did nothing more than scream and cause a general ruckus. The moon rose in the sky, and it shed a flood of light over the forest.

"They seem to be waitin' for some kind of signal," muttered Baltas.

"Maybe," said Skemtun, stepping forward and looking out onto the field. And then a warhorn sounded above the hills, its booming wail loud and terrible in the distance. It was a long way off, but it had a chilling effect.

"Did ye hear that?" Skemtun asked with a harassed look on his face.

"Aye," Baltas responded. "That wasn't one of ours."

In the distance, a battering ram, pushed by the horde, rolled out of the trees. At one point, an unfortunate orc fell in front of the machine, trapping his leg underneath. The creature screamed for help, but the wheel passed over his body, crushing him and spilling his entrails on the ground. The orcs pushed forward as if nothing had happened, stepping over their fallen comrade without a second glance.

Skemtun turned away from the ghastly sight, his stomach churning. *They're monsters, the whole lot o' them!* Skemtun set his jaw and clenched his axe handle. *I'll give somethin' to these rotten greenskins! The bloody death they deserve!*

A number of orcs carried scaling-ladders above their heads. They were crudely constructed things, masses of rope and timber, but they could get the job done all the same. They were working together in small, organized groups. There was structure... and order. In all his life, Skemtun had never seen such a sight. The rumors were right, for once, the orcs had a leader who knew what he was doing. King Nar was calculating and intelligent, and he had trained them well. As soon as the ladders were in position at the front, a horn sounded and the orcs surged forward, propping their siege ladders against the wall.

Now the dwarves scrambled to respond.

"Ready the oil!" Baltas shouted. Steam curled up from the giant vats of oil. The oil was mixed with black pitch and was designed to stick to anything it came in contact with. The stuff was deadly. Baltas raised an arm. "Pour the oil! Toss it as far as ye can, lads! Let's hit 'em where it hurts!"

Counting and swinging, the dwarves released the vats. The bubbling oil flew outwards in a dark wave, coating the attackers on the ladders and near the gate. Agonized screams rose up as the hot oil stripped away their green flesh. Most collapsed and died instantly, but others screamed and writhed on the ground. The orcs stepped back from the gates, dragging the bodies of their dead with them.

The dead bodies were kicked aside, trampled, and eventually carried off the battlefield to be stacked into a heap. Skemtun was glad of one thing. The orcs didn't use healers, as they considered it a weakness. Their fallen would be left to die and then the bodies burned.

Baltas pointed behind him to where more vats of oil stood. "Bring those cauldrons forward. We need to be ready when they come back." The soldiers did as instructed and began dragging them to wood fires set up on the walkway.

In the meantime, Baltas ordered that the catapults be readied. The dwarves had four small catapults and two larger ones. The smaller catapults were designed for lethal accuracy, while the larger ones were for hurling larger boulders upon groups who were farther away.

"Ready the *fire-spheres!*" Baltas shouted.

The soldiers grabbed the fire-spheres: large balls of compressed grass that were drenched in animal fat and then rolled in tar. The center of the ball contained a glass orb of flammable liquid which would explode on impact.

"Crank those wenches!" Baltas yelled. Soldiers placed the spheres in the smaller catapults and then cranked them back for the first volley. Just before release, the spheres were lit. Baltas eyed the catapults and nodded. He raised his hand in the air and screamed, "FIRE!"

The fiery balls glided above the walls, racing toward the orcs like swarm of hornets. The balls shattered and exploded on the ground in a deadly cascade. This made the orcs retreat even faster, for the flaming oil caught everything on fire around them. Orcs fell to the ground in flaming death.

"That helped, but now what?" Skemtun asked.

Baltas shook his head. "They've retreated back a bit, at least." He spoke quietly, so he wouldn't alarm the soldiers. "That's half our oil supplies, gone. They've got greater numbers than I've ever seen."

Skemtun feared what lay ahead, but he wasn't alone. Even Baltas seemed worried. They scanned the moving shadows in the fields below. At the edge of the forest, even more orcs emerged from the trees. *Would they ever stop?*

They kept coming. Wave after wave. The sheer number was overwhelming, incomprehensible.

The orcs started bonfires to burn their dead. The smoke coming from the funeral pyres wafted toward the mountain in a fetid cloud. Overcome by the stench, several dwarves left their posts to vomit over the wall.

After the flames died down, the orcs picked up their ladders and started pushing toward the gate again. They weaved through and set up just behind the first mass. There they paused, waiting for their signal.

Baltas raised his hand. "Load the larger catapults, men. Load 'em with the chippings!" Soldiers loaded the catapults again, this time with diamond-shaped rocks that were sharpened on both ends. Soon they were ready, and Baltas gave the command, "Fire! Fire now!"

The dwarves' second volley hurtled over the walls and into the enemy lines. The sharp rocks spun end over end, whistling through the air and crashing down on the mass of orcs below. The orcs tried to move out of the way, but they couldn't avoid the rain of death. Skemtun could hear the crunch of bones from where he stood. The sharpened stones stuck fast, impaling chests and bodies, slicing through limbs and necks. As the dust settled from the impact, more orcs stepped forward to replace the fallen. No matter how many the dwarves seemed to kill, there always seemed to be more of them.

Baltas raised his arm again. "Fire again! Don't stop! Fire again!"

More stones soared overhead. "As long as they keep comin,' I want ye to keep shootin'!" Baltas cried. He ran to the front of the parapet and grabbed a bow lying on the ground.

"Archers to the wall!" he cried. He lifted his bow and shouted, "Grab yer bows, men!"

The dwarves drew their bows and notched their arrows. The bows were exquisitely crafted weapons, as beautiful as they were deadly.

"Aim!" shouted Baltas. The dwarves drew back the strings.

"FIRE!" he ordered.

The pluck of strings resonated through the air. A cloud of black arrows flew over the horde, arcing high in the sky, obscuring the moon like a cloud of bats. The arrows swept through the front ranks, hitting their marks. Orcs collapsed, writhing in pain, arrows lodged deep in their chests. Baltas raised his arm again and screamed, "Fire!"

A second cloud of arrows rained down, but this time the orcs raised shields against the barrage. The arrows that hit their shields clattered harmlessly to the ground. Baltas raised his own bow to fire with the others. "Do it again! Again!"

Wave after wave of arrows flew from the ramparts. But it simply wasn't enough. Hundreds went down, and a thousand more poured forward to fill the gap. Horns wailed in the air, and more greenskins ran onto the battlefield, shouting war cries. The horde was enormous.

The battering ram weaved through the fields and approached the gates. Some of the orcs stopped and fired their own bows, their arrows tipped with poison. A few steps away from Skemtun, a young dwarf tried to peek down by tucking his head through the gap. Seconds later, the dwarf screamed, a black-feathered arrow buried deep in his eye. He toppled back and collapsed, the bow flying from his grip.

"Step back from the barrier!" screamed Baltas. "The wards only work if ye stay behind it!"

The orcs began to scale the walls.

"Ready the remaining oil!" Baltas yelled. Dwarf guardsmen rushed forward with the remaining oil vats. They tilted the caldrons on their mobile supports. The scalding contents poured over the orc warriors below, adding to the chaos on the ground. The terrible screams of burning orcs rose in waves.

Skemtun knew they wouldn't last long with so many firing on them at such a close range. He dropped his bow and ran to the back of the lines. Finding a torch, he picked it up and lifted it over his head.

"Grab a torch! Everyone that's not firing arrows or working the catapults *needs to grab a torch!*" Skemtun screamed.

The soldiers scrambled to comply, running back to light their torches in the braziers that kept the oil hot. Skemtun led them this time, carrying his torch like a beacon. He squeezed through the line of archers and found a gap between the protective stones on the ramparts. From there, he motioned to the men. "Don't try to hit the orcs! Just aim for where the ground looks wet!" he shouted, tossing his torch down onto the ground below.

The torch flew toward the earth, hissing and crackling, before finally reaching the oil-soaked ground outside the gate. A wall of flame roared up, blanketing their attackers with fire. Orcs screamed and fled in terror, clawing at their burning faces. Skemtun called to the spellcaster. "Strengthen the fire wall!"

A dwarf spellcaster came up behind him and raised his skinny arms. He knew what to do. *"Incêndio!"* he cried, his voice coming out in a croak.

The fire flashed a brilliant white, spreading out farther, burning higher and hotter, consuming everything in its path. *"Incêndio!"* cried the spellcaster again, his breath wheezing. Fire spread outward into the horde. Flashes of smoke appeared within the wall of fire as orcs were consumed by the flames. Burning along with their siege tools, the orcs screamed and tore at their leather armor.

"Try to destroy that battering ram!" cried Baltas, and the spellcasters renewed the spell over and over. The flames kept spreading, reaching the spot where the orcs' siege weapon lay, winding up and readying for its first assault. The battering ram was claimed by the fire. The flames ate through the wooden wheels, and the machine collapsed in a burning heap. The orcs scrambled back, retreating to the tree line.

The fire raged on. The dwarves looked down at the carnage. The air was so filled with smoke and burning bodies that it was impossible to see the battlefield. Minutes ticked by, then hours. The smoke cleared slowly, and once it did, as far as anyone could see, there was carnage and burned corpses.

Bodies, covered with blood and soot, were heaped on top of one another. Remnants of their equipment lay on the field, charred and broken. Baltas came up behind Skemtun and clapped him on the shoulder. "Ah, well done. We got 'em good."

Skemtun wasn't so sure. A few hours remained until dawn, and the orcs would continue to fight through the night and possibly the next day. But their front line had been decimated. Thousands had been killed.

Skemtun slowly lifted his lips. "Maybe there's hope for a victory after all, eh?"

Baltas smiled. "Aye, I thought it'd be tough, and it was, but this might be the worst of it. They don't have any siege equipment left, except for a few ladders. That's not enough to beat our defenses. Now we just need to withstand the siege and whittle away their forces until they give up and go home. A few months of dealin' with a siege and they'll turn around, just like they did last time. Sure, they can pound on the gates, but without proper equipment, what can they do? Maybe King Nar isn't nearly as smart as everybody says he is! Heh, heh!"

Skemtun wanted to leap up and cheer. "A victory like this is exactly what we needed. Even the dragon riders can help us now. They can get us food supplies and will spread word to our allies. We'll make it!"

"Aye, so we will," said Baltas, smiling. All around him, the dwarf soldiers on the ramparts whooped and roared and clapped gauntlets over steel-clad backs.

But then something else caught their attention. A sudden burst of shouts made Baltas turn and look beyond the battlefield. He looked beyond the smoke and still-smoldering flames. Furrowing his eyebrows, he whispered, "What in bloody 'ell is that?"

Skemtun asked, "What?"

"Just look. Look at that!" Baltas pointed a trembling finger into the distance.

Skemtun spun around. From the forest, an army of drask appeared, lumbering out of the trees, snapping at everything with dripping jaws. "Well, the drask can't scale walls," Skemtun said.

"Not that," said Baltas quietly. "Look behind 'em."

Skemtun struggled to see through the haze and darkness. He gasped when he saw what had upset the old dwarf. Another battering ram, covered with branches to camouflage its presence, emerged. As it came into view, the orcs tossed its leafy camouflage to the ground. There was a terrible clanking sound as the machine inched forward.

This battering ram was gigantic, easily twice as large as the other one that they had just destroyed. By the looks of it, it was also much better constructed. While the other machine was made of wood and ropes, this machine gleamed with iron plating and countless rows of bronze spikes. It had a giant iron head, covered in black tar and carved into the shape of a hammer.

Skemtun gasped. *The other machine was a decoy! King Nar had tricked them!* The horrible realization hit him like a fist in the gut.

The huge machine lumbered down the hillside, and into the scorched fields. Countless orcs pushed from behind. The orcs cheered as the giant ram lurched forward. The machine rolled up the ridge to the gates— no small feat for the orcs. On the horizon, the sun was just starting to rise. All their burning oil was gone, and it would take at least a day to prepare more. Half their arrows were used up, and the spellcasters were exhausted. What hope was there of keeping the orcs out of the city now?

Baltas cursed. The dwarves had played their hand too soon. With a shaking voice, he cried out, "Man the catapults! Take down that machine!" The dwarves loaded their catapults with stones and small boulders; anything they had. The stones flew into the horde below, killing dozens, but doing no visible damage to the machine.

"We'll get through it," Baltas said, his voice cracking. "We've always made it through in the past, and we'll do the same again."

Skemtun nodded and wanted to reply, but when he opened his mouth, he couldn't speak. Only a croak came out. He could see their troops shaking, beginning to falter. Any sense of bravery was gone. Fear and confusion appeared on their faces.

He forced a smile. He had to put on a brave face, for the men at least.

The ram passed through the worst of the burned areas, crushing dead bodies in its wake. Now the machine's momentum carried it forward down the hillside. More orcs ran to surround it, grunting and pushing to get it into position.

Near the back of the horde, a huge orc wearing iron chain mail appeared. There, riding a massive, armored drask, sat King Nar himself. Nar was deep in conversation with another orc. Hanging from his side was a broadsword. Magnificent black armor, decorated with polished animal skulls, encircled his barrel-like chest. The Orc King widened his jaw to reveal jagged rows of gleaming yellow teeth, each longer than a man's thumb. Even from a distance, the dwarves could see that Nar was laughing.

At dawn, the new machine reached the front gates. For a brief moment, the world hung still and all was silent. Skemtun raised a shaking hand and took a gulp from his water skin.

The dragon riders were flying directly above them now, circling in tight formation. Skemtun couldn't see their faces, but he knew what they were thinking. It was what they were all thinking. If the gates failed, they'd be annihilated.

The orcs pushed the ram into position and grabbed the ropes. They pulled back, lifting the head so high that it almost reached the battlements. Then, they let go. The gears spread open and the battering ram swung forward.

"Ram!" Baltas yelled. He raced off, shouting commands to the frightened troops.

A loud boom, like thunder, resonated through the air. The soldiers stationed above the gate lurched from side to side, stumbling backwards from the wall. The ground rattled horribly, sending two archers toppling over the sides. They were quickly torn to pieces by the orcs below.

"Look out!" screamed Baltas. "Step back from the wall!"

Another boom sounded, this time followed by a crack and low whine.

Suddenly, Kathir appeared at the top of the stairs. For a second he stood there, frozen, taking in the chaotic scene. "What's going on? Why didn't anyone call for me?" he said, his voice laced with alarm.

Skemtun turned with a horrified cry. "The orcs are at the gate! They've breached our defenses!"

Kathir rushed to Skemtun's side. "I've got to get you out of here!"

Skemtun shook his head. All around him, dwarves were paralyzed with fear.

"Boom!" went the battering ram again, striking the ancient gates. A single dent appeared in the right door, and one of the hinges ripped from its frame. The terrible tremors caused a rock-fall that spilled debris onto the battering ram and the orcs below. A cloud of dust rose up, but the orcs didn't stop their attack.

"Boom!" came another attack. A few moments later, the sound of the battering ram ceased, and the iron gates of Mount Velik collapsed.

Thousands of orcs rushed forward, overwhelming the small battalion stationed inside the gate. The orcs poured through the shattered doors. The dwarves watched helplessly as the horde stormed into their now-defenseless city.

Baltas spun around, shrieking new orders. "The walls are breached! They're coming through! We need help! Save the women and children!"

Kathir rushed to the edge of the wall and gasped. "Please, Skemtun, you've got to listen to me," he pleaded, grabbing the dwarf's shoulder. "I'm telling you, we need to get out of here now. If we don't leave now, we won't get another chance. The orcs will be coming up the stairs any minute. It's my job to protect your life! You'll die here!"

Adrenaline surging, Kathir jumped forward, trying to pull Skemtun towards the door. The madness of panic took over as it looked like they could be trapped above the doors, unable to escape.

Skemtun jerked away and grabbed his axe, raising it above his head. "I can't abandon my people. I must see this through to the end."

They heard a loud grunt behind them and swung around to see an orc hurdling up the stairs. The orc faced them with a terrible shriek. There was another one right behind him.

"It's too late, it's already too late..." Skemtun cried, swinging his axe into the neck of the first attacker.

It was over...Mount Velik had fallen.

The Temple

Far away in the Elburgian Forest, Tallin and Mugla continued onward toward the coast. The sun was bright, the air clear and cool. They flew low above the treetops, and Tallin shrouded them with a concealment spell whenever they flew over a village.

They had already been traveling for several days. This morning they would cross over the pass dividing the city of Faerroe and the Jutland River valley, about the midway point in their journey. Tallin and Mugla kept their minds warded and closed to any telepathic communication. They didn't want to risk any more unpleasant contact with the elves. Because of this, they were oblivious to the carnage wreaked upon the dwarves.

A large bird flew up from a nearby tree and almost hit them, but Duskeye swerved easily. The sudden movement took Mugla by surprise, and she yelped. "Look out!"

Tallin chuckled and steadied his aunt by grabbing her around the shoulders. "Sorry about that.

I'm used to sharp turns, but sometimes I forget that not everyone is a dragon rider."

She gave her nephew an exasperated look. "Can ye be a little more careful?"

"Sorry," Tallin said, tapping the dragon's shoulder. "Let's go a little higher, Duskeye." The dragon nodded and rose smoothly into the clouds.

"How close are we?" asked Mugla. "It's been a long time since I've traveled this far west. The countryside looks different than it did two hundred years ago."

"We're still many days from the coast," replied Tallin.

"Will the elves get there before us?"

Tallin shook his head. "No, the elves are traveling on foot. They'll arrive at the rendezvous point later than us. Duskeye flies faster than they can run, so we can take our time."

Mugla smiled. "Well, that's nice. I enjoy seein' the countryside."

Along the way, they stopped to rest and spend the night at various points. One day, they were delayed for several hours while Tallin repaired a tear in Duskeye's saddle. It rained heavily the following day, so they waited outside the city of Jutland for the storm to pass. Tallin found a dry cave for them to sleep in, and although he didn't get much rest, it felt good to lay down and relax.

Mugla stretched out on the floor, wrapped her shawl around her body, and went to sleep. Tallin was hungry but the idea of food wasn't tempting. He felt too nervous about their journey.

Soon the rain cleared, but a thick fog remained. Tallin donned a heavy wool cloak and gave his aunt a thick blanket to wrap around herself. The cold fog made flying uncomfortable, but safer for all of them.

They spoke little, except for Tallin's infrequent comments about the landscape or some village that they happened to pass. Each was sunk in their own thoughts.

Tallin seemed increasingly preoccupied, while Mugla kept anxious eyes on her nephew, waiting for an appropriate time to tell Tallin her news about Skera-Kina. The last few days had turned everything on its head. She no longer knew what to think. But instead of sharing her fears, she kept quiet, not wanting to upset him.

As the days passed, the forest became sparser, and wild vegetation covered the landscape. The remaining trees became smaller and spaced farther apart. As nightfall approached on the twelfth day, the coastline became visible on the horizon. There was a lull in the wind and the fog dispersed, revealing a bright skyline. Sea birds were visible in the distance, diving into the water to catch their dinner.

They stopped one last time to rest, camping on top of a hill. A short distance from their camp lay a tiny settlement of less than a dozen homes. Beyond the valley there was nothing but ocean, vast and wide.

The temperature dropped sharply in the evening, and after some consideration, Tallin decided to build a small fire, something that they had avoided for most of the journey since it drew attention to their location.

As the sun dipped down into the sea, the ocean became a brilliant purple streak above the dunes. Even from a distance, one could tell that the water was rough, with frothy whitecaps all across the surface. The distant sound of waves pounding onto the shore traveled inland on the breeze.

Tallin turned his head to gaze at the horizon. "It's been several years since I've been this close to the Black Sea. I'd forgotten how the ocean sounded."

"The waves are high. That means that the Lord of the Ocean is mad today," Mugla said. "We should throw some bread into the water to appease him."

Tallin chuckled. "That's just an old sailor's tale."

"It's not!" said Mugla adamantly. "There's a lot of truth in those tales. The sea has a dark temper and it would do well for ye to show some respect."

Surprised by her brusque tone, Tallin decided to listen. "Well, we have some time. Why don't you tell me one of those old sailor stories?"

Pleased with the suggestion, Mugla replied, "Good idea! What do ye want to hear?"

"Tell me about the sea," said Tallin, pulling a piece of dried meat from his saddlebags. He ate it slowly and sat down to listen. As soon as Tallin was settled, she began her tale.

"Long ago, when the land of the elves was still part of Durn and before humans walked the earth, a bountiful harvest season passed, and Saekonungar the sea god was born. Saekonungar's mother was Golka, the dark goddess of war. His father was Bannus, the jolly god of festivals. That's why the sea is so temperamental. Saekonungar's father only wanted to have fun and make merry, while his mother only wanted to fight and make war. Eventually, Saekonungar grew tired of his parent's bickering, and he left to go live in the bottom of the sea. That's why the sea god is both generous and spiteful at the same time. In one breath, he will push fish into yer net, and in the next breath, he'll crush yer boat. Sailors know this, and that's why they always spit over the stern, in order to give the Lord of the Ocean something of themselves, in the hope that the sea god will give them calm seas in return."

"Hmm," said Tallin. "Nice story. I don't remember that one from my childhood."

"Ye wouldn't have. It's a story that I learned during my travels. Dwarves are creatures of the earth, not of the sea. Our people dwell in the mountains, so the sea god is not worshipped by us, but ye should still respect him when ye are in his lands. Just because Saekonungar isn't *yer* god doesn't mean he isn't important to somebody." She grew quiet after that, drawing her blanket up to her chin. Tallin thought she'd fallen asleep.

It was dark now. Only the dim light of their small campfire illuminated their surroundings. But then she said, "I'm going to say a little prayer to the sea god tonight. I think ye should do the same. Crossing the Black Sea is difficult, even when the water is calm, and we could use the sea god's help." With that, she turned around and fell asleep.

Tallin tried to sleep, but couldn't. His mind wouldn't let him relax. *Am I doing the right thing?*

Now that they'd come so far, he felt riddled with doubt. He couldn't believe he was doing this, risking his life and his aunt's life on what now seemed like a very risky plan. After hours of tossing and turning, he finally fell into a restless sleep, troubled by dark dreams.

Tallin awoke the nest morning with the elves standing over him, shaking his shoulder.

"Wake up, halfling," said Carnesîr. "We're here. It's time to go."

Tallin sat up and threw off his blanket. All that remained of the fire was a mound of ashes. "When did you arrive?" he asked.

"Just now, as the sun was rising," said Amandila. "We ran through the night. I saw the smoke from your campfire from a distance."

"Do any of you wish to rest awhile?" asked Tallin, rubbing his eyes.

Though all of them looked weary, Carnesîr replied, "No. We are close to the end of our journey. We'll rest later, on our way to the island."

Mugla took that moment to pop up from her sleeping place, crouched behind some tall grasses.

"*Hell-ooooo!*" she shouted at the top of her lungs, and cackled when all three of the elves jumped with surprise. She had been completely covered, and she was so small that she looked like a roll of blankets.

Carnesîr's face went pale. "Mugla!" he cried, "What are *you* doing here?"

Tallin's eyebrows shot up. "You two know each other?" He hadn't expected that.

Mugla hooted, "Oh yes, Carnesîr and I go way back, don't we, ye scheming old tramp? We were in the war together. Do you remember those times? Not all of them were *good* times, mind ye." Her voice was taunting.

"She can't come with us," said Carnesîr firmly.

Tallin stood up. "Why not?"

"Yea, why not?" said Mugla with a toothless grin. "Sorry to disappoint ye, but you can't stop me. I'm coming along, whether ye like it or not."

Carnesîr blinked, taken aback. "Why, you simply can't. I forbid it!" His words trailed off in sputters and gasps.

Tallin couldn't believe what he was hearing. *Carnesîr is really upset over this—genuinely upset!*

"Oh, grow up, Carnesîr!" Mugla snapped, poking the elf's chest with her bony finger. "Ye can't stop me from coming along."

Carnesîr's face turned almost purple with rage. "How dare you speak to me so disrespectfully!"

Tallin noticed that Fëanor was smirking. Amandila covered her mouth with her hand so Carnesîr could not see her laugh.

Mugla enjoyed the elf's rising discomposure. "Ye're such a toffee-nosed gobbin. This mission is about savin' the dragons, and if we're lucky, gettin' rid of a few nasty assassins along the way. This mission is *not* about putting another feather in yer cap or pleasing yer snotty queen, do ye understand?"

Carnesîr raised a trembling finger at Mugla's face. "I refuse to allow this foul-mouthed dwarf to accompany us. I refuse!"

"Nonsense," said Tallin, "Mugla's visited the island. She knows the terrain and the location of the temple. Her knowledge is useful to me."

"Fëanor's been there, too! We don't need her to come along!" Carnesîr argued. His hands were clenched into trembling fists by his side.

"Well, it's not your decision, it's mine," Tallin said. "And I say she's coming. If you don't like it, then you can turn around and go back to Brighthollow by yourself."

Carnesîr's face turned a rainbow of colors as an internal battle raged within him. After what seemed like an eternity, he responded. "Fine," he spat. "That's perfectly *fine!* But don't blame me when she ruins this mission with her careless attitude!"

Tallin bit his cheek to keep from laughing. The elf's anger was so overblown that it was ridiculous.

"I'm going down to the dunes. I'll hire the boat." Carnesîr shot Mugla a withering stare and pushed past them, walking toward the beach.

Mugla couldn't resist sticking it to Carnesîr one last time, and shot a final insult at his retreating back. "Eh! Where're ye going in such a hurry, ye stuffy bastard? We're just starting to catch up on old times!" Tallin couldn't hold back after that and doubled with laughter.

Carnesîr ignored them all and kept walking, his back rigid with anger.

Tallin started cleaning up the camp and packing away the blankets. In the meantime, Mugla introduced herself to the other two elves.

Amandila and Fëanor were aloof, but polite, and didn't seem bothered by the fact that Carnesîr seemed to hate her. Tallin made a mental note to ask Mugla about her gripe with Carnesîr later, when they could speak in private.

At that point, Duskeye left, going back to Shesha's cave to help her guard the nest. The remainder of their journey would be by sea until they reached the island of Balbor. Tallin didn't like the thought of traveling to Balbor without his dragon, but based on Mugla's prior warnings, he knew he couldn't risk it.

They arrived at the beach an hour later. Carnesîr was waiting for them on the shoreline, near a little sailboat tied to the dock. It was still early, and they were alone on the shore.

The ocean sounded like the breathing of a giant; the unceasing roar was audible even from a distance.

"Are you sure that boat is big enough for all of us?" Fëanor asked. "It looks rather small."

"It's big enough," replied Carnesîr. "I checked it."

"Don't be so sure about that," said Mugla, prodding the elf in the ribs. "It doesn't look nearly big enough for your ego!" She cackled and slapped her knee. The other two elves giggled.

"What's... your... problem, dwarf?" said Carnesîr through clenched teeth.

Mugla smirked and tossed her hair like a young girl. "Ha! Nothing's wrong, nothing at all."

Carnesîr huffed and walked away. Tallin glanced at his aunt and noticed the crafty look on her face. She grinned back at him. She was definitely enjoying this.

They walked onto the dock and climbed into the sailboat. It was a simple vessel, with only a small cabin, a single mast that went straight up from the bow, and one big triangular sail. There were several small barrels of fresh water, but no food. Carnesîr anticipated the question and said, "The man who loaned us the boat gave us plenty of fishing poles and lures."

Tallin shrugged. He supposed they could fish along the way. Tallin moved to the back of the boat and used an oar to push the boat away from the dock. There was a hush on the dock as they moved silently into the water. Mugla sat alone near the mast. The three elves huddled together at the front of the boat. Tallin stood at the rail, looking back at the shore as they moved out to sea.

There was no turning back now.

The elves spoke in whispers, and then, only in elvish. Sometimes it looked as if they were speaking, but their mouths weren't moving at all.

None of them spoke very much, not even Mugla, who was now oddly subdued and lost in her own thoughts. "Five days," she said cryptically then spoke no further. They sailed day and night, taking turns on the night watch while the others slept. The ocean looked vast and empty.

The next morning, Tallin's stomach pinched with hunger, so he grabbed a fishing pole and tried his luck. He'd never done much fishing, but he was able to catch several while the sun was rising. He gutted the fish on deck, saving the entrails for later to use as bait. He skewered the fish and cooked it himself, using a magical flame. Mugla did the same.

Tallin offered fish to the elves. Carnesîr and Amandila refused, but Fëanor accepted one fish and ate it without cooking. Steering by the stars, they sailed for five days before the island came into view. Balbor sat on the horizon like a huge black plate. "Go north," said Mugla. "The southern coast is crawling with frigates."

Tallin changed their course and waited for nightfall before approaching the island. That night, the water darkened, and the sea became choppy. The boat rocked back and forth in the tumultuous waves. Tallin grabbed the oars and struggled to keep the sailboat steady.

Soon they were battering their way into a rising storm. His stomach began to send warning signals, and he watched Amandila jerk herself to the edge and vomit over the side. The sea was churning wildly, pounding over the deck. The water stung their faces and arms. All of them were soaked to the skin. Jagged lightning bolts flashed in the sky, and one hit dangerously close to the boat.

"It's the wards!" cried Mugla. "This boat won't take much more! We've got to get to shore!"

"We're still too far out!" said Tallin.

"I can do it," said Fëanor, his lips set in a grim line. He stood up on the deck, and raised a glowing hand into the sky.

"Sefask!" he cried out, and a bubble of dazzling white energy surrounded them. The boat steadied, and became still. Directly underneath the boat, the water was like glass. But all around them, outside the bubble, the ocean churned and boiled.

Fëanor gasped, "Grab the oars! Move quickly! These wards are powerful, and I don't know how long I can hold on!" His face was a mask of pain, and a feverish pulse throbbed at his temple.

Everyone grabbed an oar and started rowing furiously, trying to draw the boat out of the brutal current. Fëanor cried out and fell to his knees, but his spell didn't falter.

"Row faster!" cried Tallin. The boat lurched, shuddered, and moved forward. They finally reached a darkened beach on the northwestern side of the island, and Fëanor collapsed, tumbling over the side of the boat and into the water. Tallin jumped out, pulled the unconscious elf from the water and carried him to the shore.

Seconds later, Fëanor woke up in a daze, coughing dirty water.

"We made it," said Tallin. "Thank you, Fëanor."

The elf nodded and stood up. "The wards are stronger now than before. We shall have to be more careful when we leave this place."

There were no seabirds anywhere, and the beach was deserted. The night was incredibly dark, and the beach was shrouded in heavy fog. The shore was littered with brown seaweed, and wood flotsam drifted onto the surface.

"Push the boat back out into the sea," said Mugla. "Make sure that it sinks. We can't afford to have it discovered in the morning."

"But if we destroy the boat, how will we get back?" asked Amandila.

"We'll worry about that later," said Mugla. "It's more important that our presence is not discovered. Trust me."

Carnesîr gave a slight nod, and Fëanor kicked the sailboat back out to sea. It went far with a single push. He muttered a short spell under his breath, and a large wave rose up to tip the little sailboat onto its side. With another wave, the sailboat flipped over completely.

Carnesîr threw a firebolt at the upturned hull, blasting a hole in its side. The ship sank slowly to the bottom. "Let's be on our way," he said quietly, and they walked off the beach together, entering a thin forest beyond the bluffs.

"We must travel only at night," Mugla cautioned, "by moonlight. We mustn't be seen."

They traveled swiftly, only speaking out loud when absolutely necessary. The elves raced through the trees, while Tallin brought up the rear. Mugla kept up as best she could.

They made camp in the forest, stopping just before sunrise. Tallin prepared a meal from the remainder of the fish he had caught before, supplemented with some wild berries they had found along the way. They took watch in pairs, too cautious to build a campfire, despite the cold temperatures. They slept during the day under a concealment spell.

Tallin foraged what he could along the way, finding a few mushrooms and edible wild plants. He shared everything with Mugla, but overall they ate very little. He wasn't concerned with his appetite. He didn't think he could eat much, even if it was available to him. The elves seemed to eat nothing at all, although they did stop frequently to drink.

They reached the forest's edge a few days later. Outside the tree line, there seemed to be little more than scrubland. There were no villages, nor any houses, visible in the distance.

"What a desolate place this is," said Amandila after a time. "No flowers, scarcely a tree, no animals in sight. The only birds I've seen are blackbirds and crows."

"It's barren here," said Mugla, "and it just gets worse."

They started passing isolated villages. They moved quickly and kept their distance away from the homes. The sun was rising when they reached a stony valley with a massive city in its center.

The mountains around the city had been dirtied by mining, and a polluted river filled with debris snaked through the center of the valley. The surrounding fields weren't cultivated. The main temple rose dramatically on a hill in the center of the city, clearly visible from afar. The cathedral itself was a massive structure with an enormous dome.

"We've arrived. That's the capital," said Mugla quietly, pointing into the distance. Stone walls rose up in a solid block.

"What a foul city," said Fëanor. "It's even uglier than the last time I was here. I thought it was impossible for this place to get any uglier, but I was wrong."

"What's the name of this place?" asked Amandila.

Mugla shrugged. "Who knows? The high priest gets to name the city, and he changes the name as often as he desires."

"That's the stupidest thing I've ever heard," said Amandila.

"I'm sure it seems logical to them," Mugla said. "It's no use traveling at night anymore. From now on, we'll need to disguise ourselves. All of us must look like slaves and behave like slaves. No one looks twice at them in this city."

The elves shimmered, and their appearance altered. They looked shorter and scruffier, with scars on their faces. Their clothing turned shabby and faded. Their faces looked more human. They all rubbed dirt on their faces and scraped dirt into their fingernails so they looked like common laborers.

"Should we speak a certain way?" asked Tallin.

"Just use the common language. Don't worry about trying to hide your manner of speech. The majority of slaves come from the north, but the Balborites steal slaves from everywhere, so you won't draw attention simply by talking. It's *what* you say that's important. And whatever you do, don't speak to any mageborns! They're heavily warded and they'll see through your disguise. Don't speak directly to the freeborns either, unless they speak to you first. That's especially true for the women. A freeborn citizen is allowed to kill a slave for any reason; all they have to do is compensate the owner."

"What a bunch of savages," said Amandila.

"You have no idea how right you are," said Mugla. "Just be cautious, speak quietly, and keep your eyes down."

"How are we going to destroy the temple?" Carnesîr asked. "Have any of you actually thought of that?"

Tallin ignored his sarcasm. "Mugla described the temple to me in detail. We'll have the best chance of success by collapsing the main chamber. The dome is vulnerable. If we can find a way to collapse that, the structure will be rendered unusable."

"How are we going to do that?" asked the elf. "The temple is made of stone, so it's impossible to burn."

"We aren't going to burn it down," said Tallin, "but we *are* going to create a fire. A large dome, even one made of stone, is vulnerable to collapse during a fire. The dome is a natural funnel for the fire and heat. If we can get the fire hot enough, the metalwork in the upper part of the dome will fail."

"Could the dome collapse on us?" asked Amandila. "I'd rather not get squashed during this mission."

"I'll take primary responsibility for starting and maintaining the fire inside," said Tallin. "I can do it—I just need the rest of you to cover me. Mugla said that their religious services always happen at night, so if we're going to do this, we have to do it during the day, when the main temple is empty."

"This is a sensitive operation, but your plan is good... dwarf," said Fëanor, unusually supportive.

They said nothing more, and slowly, cautiously, they made their way toward the city at the bottom of the valley. They didn't approach together; instead, they broke into smaller groups. The elves went off, mixing with the crowd, talking briefly to other travelers coming into the city.

There was a short line of people waiting at the gate, including two freeborn citizens, a man and a woman. The freeborns pushed forward to the front of the line, and everyone stepped aside to let them pass.

The front gate was guarded by two armed men, but they scarcely gave Tallin a second glance. The guards were too busy staring at the noblewoman on horseback at front of the line. The woman was freeborn, wearing a bright yellow blouse.

She sat on a magnificent horse and was surrounded by at least a dozen servants. "Good day, Lady Eggert! What brings you to our fine city so early in the morning?"

The noblewoman gave him a thin smile. "I'm going to the slave market. I need a new seamstress. The last one was caught stealing, and unfortunately, I had to get rid of her. It's a shame, really. She was an excellent worker."

The woman looked back and noticed Tallin standing behind her. "Don't touch my horse, slave, or I'll beat you within an inch of your life," she warned in a vicious tone.

"Pardon, my lady," Tallin said through clenched teeth. He stepped back and walked away, resisting the urge to slap the sneer from the woman's face.

The woman sniffed loudly and glared at him.

The city gates opened and they went through, beginning their perilous walk toward the main temple. Other slaves shuffled by, their eyes clouded by fear and hunger.

They passed a busy street market selling all kinds of fruit and vegetables. The vendors stood inside the stalls, wearing conspicuous yellow shirts, while workers in drab clothing ran the stores. There were plenty of buyers and sellers, but no haggling for prices like a normal marketplace. Buyers simply chose their goods and made their purchases, paying with handfuls of wooden coins.

The main temple came into view, and they walked toward the colossal structure. Nothing prepared Tallin for how massive the cathedral really was. The walls rose up in opulent black marble; they looked like cliffs in a gorge.

Tallin was shaken. *What was I thinking? How are we ever going to destroy this monstrosity?*

"By Golka, the temple is enormous," whispered Tallin. "The cathedral of Parthos is tiny in comparison."

Mugla nodded. "It's even bigger than that. That's only the part ye can see. There's a network of dungeons underneath, with enough space to hold hundreds of prisoners. The priests send their unruly slaves there for torture. Ye don't want to get stuck down there, believe me. They're the worst dungeons I've ever seen, and I've seen a few."

Outside the temple, Mugla instructed them to pick up rags and buckets, so it looked like they were there to clean the temple. Amandila found rags, several brooms, and a lantern in a lower alcove.

They walked into the cathedral undisturbed and started to clean. There were dozens of servants already inside, cleaning the labyrinth of prayer rooms, winding hallways, and stairwells.

Tallin found a passageway that led to a huge main chamber. Tallin walked inside and found that it was much like all the rest, except that it was significantly larger than any of the other spaces, with a massive domed ceiling and buttresses trimmed in gold.

The chamber was dark and imposing in its own way. The stained glass was too dense to allow much light through, so the interior was lit with hundreds of red candles. Everything was morbidly decorated. Ornate tapestries hung on the walls, depicting horrific scenes of execution and bloodshed. There wasn't a happy image anywhere. It was all fire, brimstone, and death.

Tallin observed four tired-looking guards in one corner, playing cards. Several priests of lower rank milled about, bringing in offerings and lighting incense. Tallin looked around him carefully and saw Mugla and the elves positioned strategically at different corners of the room.

It was time for them to strike.

In the blink of an eye, Tallin drew his sword, rushing forward to plunge it into a guard's chest. The other guard jumped up in shock, scattering cards everywhere on the ground. The guard drew his dagger. Tallin blocked the knife with his sword and swung at the guard with his fist, connecting with the man's chin. The guard dropped to the ground, and Tallin jumped on him, hitting him until he was unconscious.

The priests screamed and tried to run, but the elves descended on them. The priests were poor fighters, and the elves made short work of them.

"Stop, slaves!" shouted another guard. Mugla silenced him with a well-placed lightning bolt to the chest. The guard crumpled to the floor.

The remaining guard shouted for help. Fëanor formed a ball of energy in the air, which flew forward with great speed and struck the guard, throwing him backwards and down the altar. The elf jumped on top of the man and slammed his head into the stone floor until he was unconscious.

"Start the fire!" yelled Mugla, "We don't have much time before they sound the alarm!"

Tallin nodded and lit the tapestries on fire. *"Incêndio!"* he cried out. Amandila and Carnesîr ran through the temple, collecting anything that would burn, throwing it into the center of the blaze. Tallin stayed near the fire, right below the dome. His body was shaking; sweat poured down his brow. The heat was so intense it put a gaping crack in the floor.

"Incêndio!" Tallin cried again, and the fire surged even higher. More guards tried to enter the chamber, but they were quickly dispatched by Mugla and the elves. Eventually, it was too hot inside for any guards to enter, and only the spellcasters remained.

The dome was filled with smoke. More fuel was added to the blaze, as Fëanor threw a heavy table onto the fire. They piled more and more into the flames, making a mountain of burning wood and paper in the center of the room.

But then... they came.

The Blood Masters. Three mageborn assassins, stripped down to simple loincloths, their warding tattoos gleaming in the firelight. One stepped out from behind a pillar and pointed a gleaming blue knife toward Mugla, whose back was turned.

Kudu oil, Tallin thought—the blue knives were always laced with poison. If the knife hit Mugla, she would be dead within seconds. "No!" he shouted, too late.

Tallin watched the blade fly through the air in a deadly arc, only to be deflected by Carnesîr's magical shield, just before it touched Mugla's neck. The elf saved her.

Fëanor and Amandila engaged the other two assassins in hand-to-hand combat. By then, all of the elves had dropped their glamour and were fighting ferociously using both physical and magical techniques.

One assassin stepped forward and leveled a sword at Tallin's head. Tallin ducked, evading the attack easily. But with his concentration broken, the fire began to dissipate downwards instead of up toward the dome.

Tallin kicked the assassin in the stomach, and the man rolled backwards expertly, rising back up in an instant. With a malicious grin, the assassin charged again, this time holding a poisoned knife in his hand.

Tallin nimbly sidestepped and then threw off his cloak. He swiped at the assassin's throat, but missed.

He was able to strike the hilt of the assassin's sword with the flat of his blade. The assassin howled as his sword was wrenched out of his grip.

Enraged, the assassin struck out with his knife, which sliced cleanly through Tallin's sleeve but didn't break the skin. The assassin kicked Tallin's sword-bearing hand. Tallin swore as his sword went clattering to the floor.

The assassin chuckled. "You've lost your sword, *mainlander,* but I've still got my knife. This blade is like an extension of my hand. I've just got to figure out how best to kill you." He let out a bark of laughter. The assassin's knife was smeared with so much kudu oil that the blade gleamed blue in the firelight.

I can't let him touch me with that poisoned blade! Tallin thought. In a single fluid motion, Tallin reached out and struck the assassin's face with his scabbard. The assassin stood stunned, his arm reaching up to where he'd been hit. That was all the time Tallin needed to whip his belt around the man's arm and yank it hard against his other hand that held the dagger.

The assassin's wrist scraped across the poisoned blade, opening a gash at the vein. A crimson line of blood appeared, and the man's face went white.

The assassin screamed, and the poisoned knife clanked to the ground while he grabbed his bleeding wrist. The man screamed again, his black eyes locking on Tallin's face. The poison shot through his veins faster than snake venom, and he collapsed. His body seized up into uncontrollable spasms, and thick foam began pouring from his mouth. A minute later, the convulsing stopped, and the man lay dead.

The elves were still fighting with the other two assassins, holding them at bay. Tallin turned his attention back to the fire, coaxing the flame back up to the ceiling, where the heat and smoke had become so intense that the metal sconces on the walls were melting. There was a horrible grating sound, and the walls started to crack. Parts of the roof crumbled down upon them.

"It's working!" cried one of the elves, still fighting the remaining assassins. Eventually, the other attackers fell. But their victory was short-lived. More shadowy figures solidified in the shadows, and they were under attack again. This time, they were outnumbered two to one. Tallin joined the others trying to defend against the growing number of assailants.

"We're outnumbered," Mugla panted. "Oh, by the gods... *look!*" Tallin followed her pointing finger.

Dread swept over him. She was there... in the darkness, hiding in the shadows. Skera-Kina stepped into the firelight, holding two gleaming daggers, one in each hand. She addressed Tallin in a growling voice. The assassins had quietly surrounded them, closing off the exit.

"Drop your weapons," she ordered. "You're outnumbered, and there are more of us coming."

They were trapped.

Tallin allowed his sword to drop to the floor. Instantly, one of the assassins retrieved it and screamed when the sword burned his hand. Skera-Kina shot the man a strange look and then turned to Tallin. "That's the same sword you stole from me outside the Highport Caverns." She kicked the hilt with her boot. "So you've set an enchantment upon my blade? Very clever. I'll just force you to remove it."

Tallin raised his chin. "I did not enchant the blade. It is unchanged. And I didn't steal it from you— that sword rightfully belongs to my family. My aunt crafted it herself."

Skera-Kina's eyes narrowed. "You're lying, dwarf."

Mugla sighed deeply. "He isn't lying," she said, stepping forward. Mugla looked at both of them and then leaned down and picked up the blade, holding it against her chest. The other assassins in the room stepped forward, but Skera-Kina raised her hand, ordering them to back off. Mugla handed the sword to Skera-Kina hilt-first. "Go on, take it... it won't burn ye."

Skera-Kina accepted the sword with some hesitation. "What sorcery is this?"

Mugla cleared her throat. "I was hoping for a better time to say this, but I guess this is going to have to be it." She turned to face her nephew. "Tallin, the sword's enchantment only allows for someone of my bloodline to touch it. That's why ye can both touch the blade."

Tallin's eyebrows shot up. "What?"

"It's true. Look at her. Look into her eyes. She's yer sister. Yer half-sister."

Tallin's heart thudded rapidly in his chest. Skera-Kina didn't say anything, but threw the sword to the ground with disgust.

Looking crestfallen, Mugla went and touched Tallin's cheek. "You have the same mother—my sister, Tildara. I'm sorry for keeping this secret from ye. So, so sorry." Tears rolled down her face.

Tallin looked ashen. It was too horrible to think about. Too horrible to grasp.

Skera-Kina's face was unreadable. "Who is my father then?" she asked, with steel in her voice.

"I don't know," said Mugla quietly. "It was an elf. Tildara was raped by an elf during the war—she got pregnant. I don't know anything beyond that."

Carnesîr blurted, "Now that's not fair! It wasn't really a rape. She seemed to enjoy—uh..." He froze, suddenly realizing what he had admitted. He stopped abruptly and dropped his gaze to the ground.

Mugla swung on him. "What did ye say?"

"Nothing!" Carnesîr said. The other elves didn't speak.

Mugla's mind made a sudden link. She lifted a trembling finger in Carnesîr's direction. "You! It was you! You were at Mount Velik during the war. You were part of the contingent that came to help us! You're that one who attacked my sister! Tildara got pregnant because of you! You smooth-faced, vile, *snake!*"

Skera-Kina looked back steadily and then stepped toward Carnesîr, stopping just a few steps in front of him. She looked him hard in the eye. "Is this true? Are you my father?"

The elf nodded slowly. "I guess I am."

Skera-Kina met his gaze, searching his eyes for a moment. Then she nodded and raised her arms high, plunging both daggers deep into Carnesîr's chest. Carnesîr staggered back, screaming with agony and surprise.

The other two elves jumped forward to help him, but they were swiftly blocked by a dozen other assassins.

Skera-Kina twisted the knives deeper, ignoring the spray of blood on her face. Together they crashed to the ground, Carnesîr clawing at the air. Tears were in his eyes as he spoke, "Why? Why would you do this to me?"

Skera-Kina's lips pulled back in a snarl. "Why? Because you are my father! And because you doomed me to a life of endless slavery! I will be forced to serve the temple for hundreds of years! It is *you* who are responsible, because you could have saved me—*and you did not!*"

Raising her head, she howled with humiliation and rage.

With that, she withdrew the daggers, leaving a gaping hole in the elf's chest. Skera-Kina stood up and loomed above him. "You have *disgraced* me, and given me the gift of a wasted life. Enjoy the ending to yours."

Carnesîr coughed blood and lay still.

Tallin felt sick to his stomach and he could hardly breathe. Amandila and Fëanor were crying. Mugla was trembling, unable to speak.

Skera-Kina spat on the ground. Her face and arms were streaked with blood. "Take them down to the dungeons. Find a cell large enough to hold them all. Chain the elves to the wall and pierce their ears with iron wire; that will prevent them from playing their little glamour-games on us. No one but the high priest is allowed to speak to them."

Skera-Kina tilted her chin upward and eyed Tallin carefully. "So, dearest *brother*... have you anything to say for yourself? Anything at all?"

Tallin met her gaze evenly. "You have defeated me. This is what you wanted, isn't it? Victory?"

She didn't blink or look away from him. "This is not a victory for me."

Stunned by her words, Tallin stumbled back. He looked into her eyes and saw her face stripped of emotion. There was nothing there; no spark. She was like a dead thing.

His cheeks flamed. *After everything that had happened, could he possibly feel pity for her?*

Skera-Kina leveled her gaze at Tallin. "I am a slave—a slave for life. I am a wretched creature. I shall live in bondage forever, bound to the temple until the end of my days. No matter how much violence I commit against you, you will always be victorious over me, because you are a freeborn man. Even in death, you would be the victor."

She spoke so emotionlessly that a shiver ran up Tallin's spine. He was speechless. Tallin realized he was in a state of confusion, and he felt drained, shattered.

Finally, he whispered, "You don't need to accept the world as it is."

"Spare me your pity," replied Skera-Kina coldly. "You shall need it for yourself."

Read the exciting conclusion of the *Chronicles of Tallin* in the next volume:

Kathir's Redemption

ISBN: 978-1-937361-16-7
Coming: February 2015

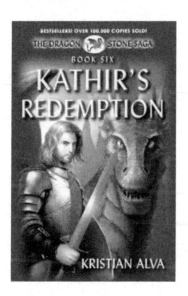

About the Author

Kristian Alva was born into a family of writers and teachers. She worked as a staff writer and a ghostwriter before publishing her own manuscripts. She now writes young adult and middle-grade fantasy full-time.

She currently lives in California with her family. When she's not writing, she enjoys reading all genres, especially epic fantasy. Find out more about the author at her official website: *www.KristianAlva.com.*

CPSIA information can be obtained at www.ICGtesting.com
Printed in the USA
LVOW04s1900020215

425350LV00037B/2222/P